Tamed by the Alien

Rebels of Sidyth
Book Nine

Sabrina Kade

WHAT'S HAPPENED SO FAR

Twenty human women have their reasons for selling their bodies to aliens for money, and no two stories are the same. It's these women who find themselves together on an assignment with some of the most feared aliens in the universe. And the circumstances for this are most unusual. Most alien races don't bring in twenty women at once. Most aliens don't say they're looking for a Chosen mate or promise they can stay with them forever. And while most women are relieved of carrying the new title of equal, some believe it's too good to be true. After all, aliens aren't kind to humans. And what little known history they have about their new buyers – the Sidyths – isn't promising.

Sidyths originate on Sidetha and are known throughout the galaxy for disrespecting females. They say they're weak. They're impulsive. They need to be tamed. If females on their homeworld don't measure up, males throw them into something referred to as "the hunt." There are a few who know the true meaning of this word, but they remain silent.

Luckily, Hethdiss isn't their homeworld, and this group of Sidyths claim they're different.

Exiled from home for refusing to follow Sidyth customs and sent to an out of the way world to fade into obscurity, their numbers are hard to guess, and their motivations are more opaque. While some aliens claim they're different, there are often homesick whisperings of the fatherland and traditions.

Sidyths are somewhat humanoid in shape, but that's where the similarities end. They're seven feet tall, blue, covered in scales, and continuously freezing without the constant presence of sun rayers or heat. They have a surprising amount of comfort, considering their exiled status. The women have a former Sidyth royal, Prince Korben, to thank for that.

Despite hospitable circumstances, however, there are still expectations.

Prince Korben didn't have twenty human females brought to Hethdiss for fun. He longed for a mate. He wanted his most trusted brothers to find mates as well. He wants to create a utopia where males and females are treated equally. Most of Prince Korben's brothers are thrilled at the idea of having a mate, (even an alien one) but most of the humans were not nearly as enthusiastic. Prince Korben promises the human females will be safe and welcome to stay if they're happy on Hethdiss, but most women have worked far too long to take the promise of an alien seriously.

Over a year has passed.

Prince Korben has his mate Blythe, the busty, feisty de facto leader of the group and the two of them now have a daughter, Kyeth. There are other successful pairings, some with children, and some without children. The Sidyths care for their mates, and most of the females accept that this is their life for the time being. There's even a real belief that they may be done working as Call-Girls forever.

But is that what everyone wants?

Life is going well at the central lair, but in comparison, the secondary seems to be at a standstill. Many of the younger, more rambunctious Sidyths have pleasure mates but aren't necessarily sure they want an alien as a Chosen mate. The women over here include what's known throughout the galaxy as State Girls; Arizona, Alaska, Dakota, and Kansas. Arizona – the leader – used to not believe in love, but Drozass has changed all that. She's still desperate to keep her family together, but she wants the rest of her companions to find happiness the same way she did.

Alaska, however, isn't looking to follow Arizona's orders. Which is odd for her, because she's so used to doing whatever Arizona tells her. Alaska doesn't believe choosing a mate will lead to happiness. After all, even back on Earth when she did follow orders, she ended up as an Intergalactic Call-Girl. She's willing to have a pleasure mate – Taylis – but doesn't think it's a good idea to expect anything more than that. However, she's shocked when out of nowhere, Taylis suggests they become official mates. She's almost excited… until she realizes the only being more professional than her, may be Taylis.

This is where *Tamed by the Alien* begins.

PROLOGUE

ALASKA

I don't like change. Let me reiterate. I. Do. Not. Like. Change. Once I'm on a schedule, I don't care what it is; I'm into it. It can be something I love. Something I loathe. Doesn't matter. As an Intergalactic Call-Girl, I don't expect to practice mindfulness or to appreciate the little victories in life. And honestly, I don't mind not being in charge. I'm twenty-seven, and I'm damn proud to have made it this long with someone I trust with my life – even if I don't necessarily agree with all her decisions. Arizona has always been known to take charge. She's always told me, Kansas, and Dakota to never fall in love. *Open your legs but close off your hearts*. It made sense to me. It still does, honestly.

Except now Arizona has done the unthinkable and fallen in love with a client – a Sidyth.

She's happy. Honestly, I barely understand the concept. From what I know, a lot of terrible things happened to her – including

I

being tricked by another Sidyth. But lately, she's all smiles. It seems like a joke to me because Arizona is telling Dakota and Kansas that she wants to see them as happy as she is with her alien mate. I don't know how either of them feels about the situation, and I'm not even sure if I care because I'm sure as shit not going to fall in love.

I should have known it was only a matter of time that Arizona would let me down. After all, everyone else has. My stepdad's friend took me away and forced me to sign a contract – giving my life aliens. I didn't bother fighting. My stepdad's friends were mean. It was easier not to fight. So I signed the papers to get away from them.

And now, here I am on Hethdiss with nineteen other Intergalactic Call-Girls.

Arizona's the one person I thought I could trust to guide me, and she's changed the rules. If I ever get out of this assignment, I'll never trust another person again.

As it is, however, I have nowhere else to go. As far as anyone knows, this assignment could go on for another few months, years, or forever. The leader of these Sidyths? Prince Korben? He says we can stay here if we find a mate. *Choosing* is what they call it. Talk about some grade A *Avatar* shit. I'm not Choosing a mate. I don't want to.

But I guess if Arizona forced me to... I wouldn't have a choice. She's the one who's always called the shots, after all.

When we first arrived on Hethdiss, I remember keeping close to Arizona, Dakota, and Kansas. We were all looking around after the Todas dropped us off. I dealt with whatever came my way because that's what the look on Arizona's face told me to do after I left her on the ship with a Todas alien. I kept close to the back of the group, not wanting to interact with anyone, and biding my time until I received the next order from Arizona.

We were introduced to the Sidyths – who don't exactly have an excellent reputation across the stars, especially when it comes to females. On their planet Sidetha, females cannot refuse a male. In any way. If they want pleasure, they can steal it. If they want a mate, they can force a female to squeeze them. (Yes, to claim a mate, females squeeze their males until they pass out. Yum.) If males don't want a female's attention, they can have her sent to something called a 'hunt.' I had a friend sent there. Washington. I don't want to talk about it.

But the Sidyths away from their homeworld weren't terrible. Their prince took a liking to Blythe, one of the bustiest chicks I've ever seen in my life. He kept her in his room, while the rest of the females were sent to the Gathering Room. I guess it wasn't terrible, either. No one took advantage, or tried to steal pleasure, and after a few days, Blythe finally convinced her little prince that human females weren't cattle he could keep cooped up until we decided we would fuck one of his supposed brothers.

By the time I reunited with the rest of the girls, I started to think that maybe things on Hethdiss wouldn't be so bad. I couldn't remember the last time an alien hadn't tried to fuck me within the first twenty-four hours of an assignment, let alone a week, so I was open to seeing what was up. Arizona didn't give us many orders, anyway. Some alien named Drozass already paid way close attention to her. She was fucking him. Dakota and Kansas were fucking aliens, too. And one look from Arizona let me know that I better fall in line and do what I'm supposed to do.

That night, we were separated once again; and it hurt more than usual. I didn't enjoy the company of York or Ellis, the workout twins, or even Krista. I just wanted my State Girls – Arizona, Dakota, or even Kansas in a pinch. I missed Arizona telling me what to do. I didn't like freedom. So honestly, I was looking to take the edge off when I felt something – or rather – someone staring at me. I lifted my head.

A Sidyth was guarding the opening to the Gathering Room, but it wasn't one of the usual suspects. I was used to the old one with silver streaks in his dark hair or the one with a mask over his mouth. Even the large, overly muscled one wasn't there. This one was different. Leaner. Younger. Unable to help myself, I lifted my head higher, trying to put a name to the face. His hair was longer in the front than in the back, and his chin surprising prominent.

And he looked right back at me.

A few of the other females in the room must have noticed the difference as well because they chatted loudly behind me. But for some reason, I couldn't pull my attention away from the new Sidyth. His skin was lighter blue than most of the others, and though he was lean, it didn't mean he was any less muscular. There was an intensity in his golden cat-like eyes that didn't let me look away. Arizona wouldn't have wanted me to, anyway.

He cocked his head to the side slightly, almost as though acknowledging the fact that he's staring at me. And I at him, I guess. But I notice he still didn't look away. I assumed he wanted me to fuck him. More and more of the females were pairing off with the Sidyths at the time. I remembered how much I desperately didn't want to fall behind. I rose up from the floor and smoothed out my tiny black skirt and sauntered in his direction.

Finally, he blinked. He crossed his thick arms tightly over his broad chest, and part of me wondered if he was going to walk away. I almost couldn't picture it at the time, but I swear now, looking back on it, he looked as though he considered walking away. His golden eyes dipped down to my toes and then flicked back up to my blonde hair in an instant, and then he blinked again.

He didn't leave from his spot.

My heart thudded heavily against my thin, black top, and I did everything to calm it, remembering Arizona's words. Keep calm. Don't be desperate. Give the client what he wants — nothing else.

I stopped a few inches away from the alien, tilting my chin to meet his eyes. He's tall, but not overly so. I allowed myself the liberty of drifting my attention up and down his frame just as he did to me. He licked his lips, slicking a long, and shockingly thin-forked tongue across the surface.

"What is your name?" he asked. He attempted to sound disinterested, but I'm the queen of disinterest, so I didn't believe for a second that he didn't already want me.

"Alaska."

"What is your real name?"

His question took me off-guard. My real name. That's something I never spoke about with anyone. My girls know – Arizona, Dakota, Kansas, and Washington, but no one else. And I intended to keep things that way. "My real name is whatever you want it to be."

A frown flickered across his sharp features, and a forked, scaled tongue worked out from his lips once again. He thought he could catch me off-guard. And I suppose that he did. But I'm already back to my composed self. Clients like it when I'm composed. Or that's what Arizona drilled into me.

"You want to come to my lair?" he asked next.

I shrugged and glanced over my shoulder. Krista, Rhyan, and the workout twins were in one corner. They didn't care what I did. Layla, Celeste, Sloane, and Phoebe were in another corner. They sure as shit didn't care what happened to me. And Blythe was off with her alien mate. Ellis and York might have been, too. Either way, they wouldn't have cared.

No one cares about me here.

"Do you want pleasure?" I asked the alien.

"Prince Korben says we're supposed to ask."

"You don't have to ask me."

His golden eyes widened. Now I'm the one who's caught him off guard. He lifted a hand to his mouth and coughed quietly into it before lowering it back to his side. "We are supposed to ask."

I hummed to myself but shrugged. "If you are asking if you're allowed to fuck me, the answer is yes."

He hissed under his breath, flicking his attention back to my eyes. "You are not going to ask my name? Who am I? What I am like?"

I shrugged again. "I don't think it matters, does it?"

He frowned. "No. I suppose it does not."

He turned around then, glancing once over his shoulder as though expecting me to follow him. And of course, I did.

His lair wasn't anything unusual. A single bed with a single blanket. A dirt opening with a dusty, off-white curtain for privacy. The scent of a lonely male jerking himself off one too many times before sleeping. And the heat. Fuck, the temperature was incredible. Sun rayers in every corner – basically acting as fans, only instead of emitting fresh air, they emitted heat and light. I broke out into a sweat within moments and wiped at my brow.

"It is hot for humans, yes?" the male asked.

"Doesn't matter."

"Why?" He cocked an eyebrow at me, but his expression quickly relaxed when I immediately stripped off my skirt and tank.

I stood naked before him, waiting for his next move. But for a while, he merely stood in front of me. Almost as though he was unsure about what to do. I allowed my mind to drift. I wondered if Arizona was fucking her alien. I wondered if Dakota and Kansas were doing the same.

I wondered if Washington was still alive, having somehow survived the hunt.

"Do you not like what you see?" I asked.

He swallowed hard. "I did not realize alien females would be so easy."

"They're not. But I am."

The male frowned. "When I touched one of your companions, she grew upset. I thought humans were afraid of us. You appear fragile." He stepped up closer. "Aren't you afraid that I'm going to hurt you?"

"You can hurt me if it pleases you."

A strangled sound escaped his lips. "You are not serious."

"Try me." I threw out my arms, daring him to do something. Throw me around. Bite me. Squeeze me. I didn't care. I still don't. Not really.

My closest friends say I'm like a robot. They say it like it's supposed to be an insult, but I don't think they could be further from the truth. I take it as a compliment. I'm not as good as Arizona, but I am a damn good star hussy. I let aliens do what they want with me. They tip me well when I do. That's what I like — making extra credits and giving them to Arizona. Seeing that pleased look on her face. But I guess she was also confused.

"I can't believe you let him do that to you," she'd say, shaking her head at my bruises after a particularly rough assignment with pre-pubescent Drakens.

"Are you happy about the money?" I'd ask. She'd nod.

That was enough to keep me going.

"I'm not going to hurt you," a new voice said, breaking my concentration. After a few blinks, I realized that the alien was standing closer to me. His large hands wrapped around my hips. His expression was almost as detached as mine, but he's faking it. A room doesn't smell like sex unless a dude really wants pleasure any chance he can get it. He has wants. Needs. He has emotions.

What a shame.

"Well, Sidyth, if you want to, you can," I said in a low voice.

"My name is Taylis."

"I'm sure it is. Are you going to ask me to be your mate?"

He shook his head. "I don't want a mate. Too much trouble."

My expression shifted. Huh. Now, that was a surprise. Suddenly, I found myself looking at the Sidyth – Taylis – with a surprising fondness. He's not looking for a mate? That's good.

Because no one is going to tame me.

CHAPTER 1

ALASKA

Present Day...

ARE SMILES SUPPOSED TO BE ANNOYING? I DON'T THINK SO. BUT every time I see Arizona, Dakota, or Kansas smile, I want to start gouging my eyes out. I'm not a violent person, at least, I don't think so, but I find myself less in control of my emotions lately. Arizona's staring up at her Sidyth – her *Chosen mate* – Drozass like he's the most fantastic thing in the world. She used to look at all her clients like that, but now, that star-struck look is reserved only for him.

It's driving me crazy.

Hoping she doesn't notice me, I duck behind a cluster of dirt in the hallways underground where the Sidyths live, and fortunately for me, Drozass and Arizona obliviously stride past. They must be heading back to their lair. There was a time where

Arizona always knew where we were. I thought she could smell us or something or had a sixth sense to make sure her girls were okay. But lately, she's on a different planet. Drozass is gently rubbing Arizona's stomach while she bats away his hand.

I narrow my eyes, my anger escalating. I need to hit something. To scream. Once Drozass and Arizona are out of sight, I sprint down the halls, desperate for fresh air. I don't care who I must see, so long as I don't see Arizona's smile. *That smile.* She's happy. She's not supposed to be. Everything she's ever said to me is a lie when I see that smile. She told us to never fall for a client. She told us never to trust them. Well, apparently that meant for everyone but her.

The Gathering Room at the central lair is more pleasant lately. More and more babies wandering around and less single Sidyths looking for something to wet their dick. Most of them don't even bother looking up when I stride into the room, never mind that I'm having a good hair day and managed to pluck my eyebrows by hand which took almost a full hour. No one cares. Of course, they don't. Honestly, sometimes I don't even know why I bother trying to look good. I have a client, and he fucks me, and the sex is incredible. He probably wouldn't care one way or the other so long as there was hole waiting for him at the end of the day.

But it still hurts to have lost so many of my girls to Sidyths. I don't see what makes them so great. They're seven feet tall, but what humanoid aliens aren't these days? They're blue. Blue's a safe color. A decent color. But nothing special. I guess their iridescent scales are kind of different, but after a year on Hethdiss, I look at them more as belonging to Edward Cullen standing out in the sun, than something to ogle. And yet, somehow, they've drawn in almost half of the females on assignment.

Blythe.

York.

Ellis.

Phoebe.

Sloane.

Celeste.

Layla.

And Arizona.

All mated and either with child, with *a* child, or trying like crazy to get a bun in the oven.

I don't want that. I'm used to not wanting that.

I'm just not used to not wanting that alone.

I expect Arizona to be standing right here next to me and snickering about how these bitches are so stupid for getting themselves knocked up by an alien. I expect Dakota to be giggling at Kansas' snarky comments. And I expect all of them to be laughing about how I'm just like a robot and they want to see if I'm an android. But they're not here. None of them are. Kansas is with Dash, and Dakota is with Cade. They're both young Sidyths who continuously like to fight each other to impress females or themselves. And Arizona is smiling like crazy and trying to get herself knocked up by an alien.

We used to laugh about things like that. On one assignment we tried coming up with book titles if we ever got back to Earth. We'd all write erotic alien novels, and we'd joke about who could come up with the craziest title.

Knocked up by Astronaut.

Turned on by the Penis Pirate.

Aroused by the Alien Aristocrat's pet.

But no. Now I'm sulking into the Gathering Room with none of my friends by my side. A lot of the mateless females are looking at me. My temperament has changed from blasé to bitchy over the past few months, and I know they're wondering if there's anything they can do to help.

Ryhan and Krista end their conversation and lift their heads, sending cautious smiles in my direction. I consider going over because 1) I don't think they have mates and 2) I'm pretty sure they aren't pregnant. I wouldn't mind talking to some reasonable girls on this assignment, so despite feeling like I don't belong, I cross the floor bustling with babies and toddlers, and take a seat on the floor in front of them.

"You look like you could use a friend," Krista says.

My lip curls. "I have friends."

She chuckles. "Ones who aren't always fucking aliens."

"They're not always fucking aliens," I say, already beginning to think coming here was a big mistake. Krista means well, but she's pissing me off. Some of the girls like to see if they can pull some emotions out of me. But I don't fall for their tricks so easily anymore.

The two shrug to themselves, but if they're expecting me to join the conversation, they've got another thing coming. I'm happy to sit with some single ladies, but my heart still aches for my family. Arizona. Dakota. Even Kansas, who I can't stand most of the time. Because they never made me feel like it wasn't okay being who I wanted to be. I don't like to lead. I like to follow. Following has always been easier for me, and now that I have no leader, I don't know what to do with myself. I feel lost. Empty.

When I'm with Arizona, I don't have to feel that way. She keeps me in line. She keeps me neutral. She tells me what to do, and I fucking do it. It's always been that way. Even when she invited me to join her on creating her family, I only agreed because it seemed like the easiest thing to do. Arizona liked my hair, my height, and my voice. I felt flattered. Special. Needed. But mostly, I agreed to be with her because it was easier than saying no, fighting with her, only to join anyway.

Under Arizona's thumb, I didn't have to think about where I was going, what I was doing, or who I was doing. Arizona told. I did. Our alliance was a lethal one because Arizona would do anything, and I mean *anything* to protect us. And I would do anything she told me. It was a comfortable existence. I never thought about saying no to Arizona about anything. At least not until she fucked up everything and we lost Washington in the process.

There's no such thing as happiness unless someone's ordering me around. Otherwise, I'll have to think for myself. Think about the consequences and rewards. I prefer someone do all of that for me. I miss Arizona, but I hate that it feels like she's abandoned me for someone else. Someone she said I could never think about including in my life. She said never to trust, fall for, or love clients. I did what I was told. I shut off my heart.

But because the rules have changed for her, she thinks they should change for all of us.

She wants all of us to be happy, which means Choosing a mate.

And there's only one option on the entire planet of Hethdiss who I can picture doing this with.

Standing without a word to Ryhan or Krista, I decide I've had enough conversation for the time being. Their eyes both widen when I hastily depart, but of course, they don't call out to me. They don't have mates now, but they're coming to realize they should find one. And soon. And if I'm going to have any chance of staying here with Arizona and the rest of the girls, I'm probably going to have to do the same thing. Some days, I'm still not sure what would be best for me, though. Am I prepared to stay on Hethdiss? Play wifey to a Sidyth so I can stay close with the only people who understand me? Or should I leave? Cut my losses and try to live my life alone?

I don't have many great fears, but I suppose I do have one.

If I leave Arizona, who will be my new leader? And will she (or he) be anything like her?

Despite Arizona's annoyingly happy smile, I want to stay with her. But I don't want to stay with Arizona as she is *now*. I want her to go back to Arizona as she was before Drozass started bothering her so much. Forcing so many of his expectations on her. Arizona isn't supposed to be a wife and mother. She's supposed to oversee the State Girls. The only family I've ever known. Just like my stepdad, she controlled every aspect of my life. She told me who to fuck, when to fuck them, and for how long. At first, I tried to grump about it, to see if she would bend, but Arizona never fell for any of it. I could scream, cry, kick, and bitch. Orders didn't change. It was comforting to know I couldn't wriggle my way out of a situation. It only took a few weeks, and Arizona's words became orders I couldn't refuse.

I shouldn't make it sound so amazing because it wasn't. Not always. But it was better than thinking I could ever cry or charm my way out of anything.

I was strong because I knew Arizona was stronger.

When I return to the opening of the central lair, my attention drifts to the secondary refuge. All four of us State Girls reside there now, but for some reason, it still feels like a rift came between myself and the others when the Todas separated us. It was only a week, but something changed in my relationship with Arizona, Dakota, and Kansas. I had Kansas, sure, but I couldn't really stand her then, and I can't stand her now. I hate how she disrespects Arizona. She fights her about everything. If she wants to fight so bad, why did she agree to be a member of her family?

When I'm about to cross onto the grass, my heart quickens when I notice a familiar shape heading in my direction. The form isn't alone... it never is. But I am happy to see Arizona's out and about, and I guess not planning to spend her entire day fucking her alien mate. Her dark eyes widen when they meet mine, but I'm still not sure if I'm ready to talk to her. Arizona thinks Taylis has something to do with me not speaking to her, but that's bullshit. I'm the one who made that decision. I don't want to talk to her. Don't want to see her. And though it bothers me that she's still wincing when she walks for some reason and her one wrist is bandaged, I don't ask why.

Drozass wraps an arm possessively around her shoulders as though they're the ones who are family, and not Arizona and me. And it makes me mad. But before I have a chance to pretend I don't see them and head back to the lair, she calls out to me.

"Alaska, come on."

I stop, glancing over my shoulder, and her short, brown legs are pumping to catch up with me before I try to hide in the maze of tunnels in the central lair.

"You have to talk to me at some point. I don't know what he told you, but you have to talk to me, dammit."

I frown, wanting to argue with her. She still thinks this is about Taylis.

Taylis. He's nothing to me. Less than nothing. He's a body. He can do whatever he wants to me because that's how things work. Or that's how they're supposed to work.

I lift my foot, prepared to walk away, but something shifts in Arizona's voice.

"*Talk to me.*"

My leg drops. It's not a request or a question. It's a damn order, and one I can't easily ignore. The only person who holds more power than Arizona is a client. And Taylis is nowhere in sight. I usually could care less about what he's doing, but I could use him right about now to avoid this. He would know I don't want to talk to Arizona. He would ask me to come with him. And he could use his power as a client to override any orders Arizona tries to give. But he's not here.

I swallow hard.

Arizona thinks it's complete and utter bullshit that I do everything she says without asking, but never actually put in a formal complaint for me to stop. She says I need to stop looking to her for all the answers, and maybe she's right in a way. But I don't know what to do with myself. It's been so long since I've thought about doing things I want to do and not doing things I don't want to do. If Arizona officially cuts ties with me, what would I do with myself? Would we remain friends, or would it be too painful? And what about Taylis? If I didn't have any formal reason to keep a client, would I stay with him because it would be easier?

Just the idea of making all these decisions makes my heart pound, and Arizona's mate rumbles something in his deep, soothing voice. Out of the corner of my eye, I notice her pull away from his grasp and rush towards me. I don't want to talk. I don't want her to cut me loose or set me free or let me fly. I want her. I need her. I don't know who I am without the State Girls or Arizona.

But I still yank myself out from her grasp when she attempts to touch my shoulder.

"Alaska," she says in a low, warning tone. "Where have you been lately? I haven't seen you in over a week. Do you think that's something I'm okay with?"

I shake my head, feeling my mouth go dry. Arizona doesn't like it when we don't check-in. Even when we're with clients, she wants to know that we're being treated well. She wants to know what we're eating and how much. She wants to know what we're doing with the clients and if it's something we don't like, is the client asking, or forcing? And if we're doing something, are we getting paid well? Are we being tipped?

For the first time since we started working together, I didn't check-in. Something hurt Arizona in the woods, but I don't know what. I didn't want to know what. And honestly, I didn't care. She had Drozass to take care of her. And kissass Dakota and annoying Kansas. Fine. She had her friends. She had her family. She didn't need me. She was so far detached; she didn't even know the reason I ignored her had nothing to do with Taylis. I decided on my own. I never make decisions on my own, but after hearing about her Choosing Drozass as a mate? I didn't want to talk to her. Didn't want to face her. She'd gone against everything she ever told me, and she expected me to be okay with it because I'm Alaska.

The robot girl.

I don't think Arizona appreciates, or even understands how difficult this was for me. How difficult it still is. But in a way, I'm proud of myself. I see it as a test run for the inevitable. Arizona is going to cut me off. I'm going to have to start making decisions on my own, and I'm going to have to find a way not to have an anxiety attack every time it happens. It sucks that it's such a massive thing, but Arizona's controlled a large portion of my life, and my stepdad and his pervert buddies controlled the rest. This is the first time I've had to do something on my own.

And when I told myself I wouldn't face Arizona, she would have to meet me first, it… felt kind of good. For once, I wasn't stressing myself out about whether she would be pleased with me or not. I just thought about what I wanted to do. And as hard as it was, I'm still alive. It wasn't impossible. It was a huge step. It still is.

I decided without Arizona's approval.

"*Speak to me,*" Arizona says, using the voice that makes the hairs on the back of my neck stand on end, even with endless blonde waves shielding them from her view.

"What do you want me to say?" I ask, lifting my chin high enough that she can't meet my eyes without standing on her tiptoes. I know our height difference is something that bothers Arizona. She's our leader, but she's the shortest one out of the four of us.

"What did he say to you?" Arizona goes on, crossing her arms. Drozass stands behind her, saying nothing, and I almost wish Arizona would tell him to piss off and that this conversation has nothing to do with him, so he shouldn't even be here. But of course, she doesn't think that way. Not anymore.

"Who?"

"You know who," she hisses. "Taylis. Did he tell you to stay away from me?"

"No."

"I don't believe you."

I lower my chin slightly. "You should. Because I know better than to lie to you."

Her expression shifts, and her dark eyes dart over to Drozass for some reason. Like he has the fucking answers. *Don't look at him. Look at me*, I'm hissing inside my head, but of course, the words never leave my lips. I may have made one decision on my own, but I'm not going to pretend I'm putting together a sort of mutiny.

"Then, why?" Her expression is confused, but her tone remains strong. "Why wouldn't you come to see me? Why didn't you come to see me?"

I shrug. "Dakota and Kansas said you were okay. I figured they could handle it."

"I needed you."

"You should have seen her—" Drozass starts.

"Don't you dare act like this has something to do with you," I hiss. "Don't you dare."

Arizona's eyes widen. She's not used to hearing me sound so passionate around clients. "He is my mate." Her voice is still calm and steady. "He was there for me when you weren't."

"Well, then I guess he can continue being there for you while I'm not." I spin on my heel, heading back towards the second lair, and part of me hopes Arizona will come running after me. She hasn't seen me for over a week. This wasn't a routine check-in. I want to turn and see her hobbling after me, wincing in her pain because she feels a need to check on me. A need to care for me. I need someone to care for me.

But she doesn't come.

"Are you all right?" a soft voice prickles against my ears right as I'm about to head back into the secondary lair. Light blue eyes stare up at me from behind strawberry blond streaks. *Taya.* The frightened little mouse who barely speaks. She must feel comfortable because her mate stands right beside her. Wixlass. They call him Wix. I narrow my eyes at him before dropping my chin. "I saw you speaking with Arizona. She's been looking for you. She wanted to make sure—"

"Stay out of it." I keep my voice low so as not to piss off her mate, but I guess my words are no less icy in her ears. She nearly winces, curling up into the arms of Wix who shoots me a glare that could melt the ice I've just shot in his mate's direction. "If Arizona asks about me, say nothing. How about that?"

She nods carefully, still obviously shaken. I resist the urge to roll my eyes. All these females are curling up and listening to every word their man says to them. For some Intergalactic Call-Girls, this would be a dangerous move. Aliens who buy females aren't precisely the type who take mates. But then again, I've only been on two assignments that have lasted as long as this one. And neither one was pleasant. This assignment doesn't feature an alien race who ages differently than humans, so a full year is nothing but a few hours for them. But despite the Sidyth's kindness, I refuse to give in. I don't want to look like Arizona. I don't want to be like punkass Taya who should be turning to her girlfriends rather than a client for comfort.

Thankfully, Wix is intelligent not to say anything to me as I sweep past, and my heart aches at the idea that Arizona isn't following me. Knowing her and Drozass, they're probably at the central lair, checking out the babies and planning some future with white picket fences on a planet where it's always raining, and the grass is purple. She's lying to herself if she thinks this is going to work. I trust Arizona about so many things, but I refuse to believe her about this. I think deep down she's afraid to reflect too much on it. She's afraid to talk about anything other than Taylis as being the reason I haven't seen her. She knows she's losing my respect. She knows this family she's worked so hard to build is falling apart.

But she doesn't give a shit because she's not the one who's miserable.

That's fine, I suppose. I've never really known true happiness or sadness, joy or grief. I only know what I'm told. My stepdad would say which of his friends I would hang out with. My stepdad's friends would tell me what they wanted me to do to them. Aliens told me the best way to stay alive. Arizona told me who and what to do. My life as an Intergalactic Call-Girl isn't that much different than my life back home.

But this? This is different.

I needed you. That's what Arizona said. As much as I want to believe her words, I have a hard time understanding them. My biggest question is why. Why would she need me? She had Drozass. She had Dakota and Kansas. And I'm sure some of the other women went to check on her. She doesn't need me. She needs to control me because she's afraid. She's worried just like I am. We're all afraid that things are changing. That this assignment is different. Babies and mates… seeing all of this shouldn't bother me. But it does. It's different. It's *too* different. The smiles are what do it for me. I'm used to forced pleasure. I'm not used to happiness.

It freaks me the fuck out.

I take a seat in the hallway of the secondary Gathering Room, not wanting to talk to anyone. I should have gone to the woods, but after whatever ordeal Arizona went through, both lairs are on high alert, and no female can go anywhere without a Sidyth escort. And I know who would want to come with me. And as frustrating as my relationship with Arizona is, my one with Taylis is almost as much. We've been pleasure mates for over a year, and yet I don't feel anything.

At least, I don't think I do.

Sometimes I wonder what would happen if I woke up and did feel something for Taylis.

That would really fuck shit up.

CHAPTER 2

ALASKA

Fuck the high alert.

After deciding that sitting around in the halls is something a drunk, stoner college freshman would do, I decide to do something else. On my own, I might add. I went to the woods after all. I'm twenty-seven. I'm a grown-ass woman, and if I want to go out, I will. I don't need permission from Arizona. Or Sidyths. No. If I want to go out, I wait until no one's paying attention and slip out beyond the borders so I can breathe again. So I'm no longer feeling suffocating by the happy couples and screaming children. The woods feel odd this far out, but Exer and York and Azan go out there all the time. Whatever happened to Arizona must have had something to do with her being stupid — not the Sidyths being on high alert.

I shouldn't be surprised if something did attack her in the woods.

But the thought does make me hesitate about heading even further away from the comfort of the lairs.

Arizona would probably have a fucking fit if she knew what I was up to. Not that I should give a damn what she thinks. She said we couldn't trust the Sidyths. She said we should only provide them with pleasure, and nothing more. She said to never fall in love. Well, she broke all her rules the moment she returned in Drozass' arms and proclaimed they were officially mates. I always saw Arizona as an older sister – someone looking out for me. And though looking back on it, I was stupid to think we could spend the rest of our lives together; it still hurts to think that after this assignment, I may never see her again.

Despite what others view as a cold demeanor, I do have emotions. I do hurt. And I'm hurting right now. No matter how much I hate spreading for aliens, I loved knowing I could check in with Arizona and the rest of the girls. That no matter how hard I had to fight to hold back the tears, I could calm myself around the others because that's what they expected from me. Cold as ice, Alaska. My given name. Maybe Arizona knew it made sense even before I did. But that's beyond the point. Even if I wanted to cry those first few months or on nasty assignments, I could compose myself for the sake of keeping everyone else calm.

There would be days Arizona's comments about my dismissive behavior would rub me the wrong way. Kansas always rubbed me the wrong way. She still does. She was the whole reason Arizona started thinking about aliens falling for clients. She would listen to Kansas' dumbass stories about the training center where she recruited her, and I swear I could see the wheels turning in her head. She considered the possibility. She thought about getting away from our line of work even before we arrived on Hethdiss. Maybe she won't admit it, but I saw it. I saw the way she changed over the months she spent with Drozass. I saw how she changed after she left Washington behind on Sidetha. She wanted love.

Now she has it. Even if she's not entirely sure she can hold on to it, she doesn't care anymore.

Even temporary happiness is better than no joy at all.

As much as I wanted to fall for the fantasy, I couldn't.

My stepdad, his friends, Arizona, and the aliens I've been stuck with over the years have hardened me.

To me, no happiness is better than having temporary happiness stripped away.

Remembering this, I trudge further into the woods. It's still early. The hot pink suns are directly overhead, so that leaves me plenty of time to head back to the lairs. I wish Arizona had come with me. Or even Taylis would be nice right about now. I barely think about my life before Hethdiss or being kidnapped by one of my stepfather's friends for that matter. If I could go back to Earth right now, I'm not even sure if I would. And that's fucking depressing. My only family, the only good I've ever known is with Arizona, Washington, Kansas, and Dakota. They aren't perfect, but they love me more than my stepdad ever did. My stepdad only used me to win over his creepy-ass friends. Once Mom died, he had no reason not to do anything he wanted with me. And so he did. He never gave me a choice. It was never an option. I just dealt with it. I dealt with him, and I dealt with Arizona. But I'll still believe with my dying breath that she cared about me. She probably still does.

And that's the only reason I'm not sprinting to the high hills to get away from everything.

I don't want a mate — too much trouble.

Taylis' voice startles me violently back to the present. *Why the hell am I thinking about that? And why him? Why now?* It doesn't matter to me or not whether he wants a mate. I shake my head hard, trying to clear the young, grumpy alien's face and voice out my mind. But it's no good. I don't know why, how, or when, but at some point, Taylis became… *okay.* Maybe it's because he never pushes me. He made it clear from the beginning that he's not looking to Choose a mate, and he's stayed true to that promise for as long as I've known him. And that's always brought me some comfort.

Except for now. Right now, standing alone in the woods, his words prickle somewhere in the back of my mind. Maybe it's all the happy couples and the babies. Maybe it's the fact that I'm losing Arizona to a Sidyth. Or perhaps it's… I don't know. Even if I wanted to Choose an alien, *which I don't*, Taylis isn't interested in a mate. Not a human female, anyway. He made that pretty clear. Despite his disgust though, he sure doesn't have a problem fucking a human female.

I pinch my eyes shut, hating that I'm going down memory lane.

It's a place that would be best left alone.

"Do you ever think about it?" My voice was hesitant that night, vulnerable after a shockingly enjoyable back-to-back orgasm. Taylis was laying on the floor, staring up at the ceiling, and even at my words, he couldn't bring himself to turn in my direction. He was still breathing hard, idly playing with his consistently hard dick. "Chosen mates," I clarify carefully. "Do you ever think about it?"

"I think about it all the time."

"Really? But I thought you said—"

"Not with a human female." He reaches across the space between us and awkwardly pats my bare thigh. "I know that a lot of my brothers are fine taking an alien for a Chosen mate, but I simply do not believe that is for me." He frowns suddenly,

removing his hand. "Have you found someone you'd like to Choose as a mate?"

"Me? Choose a mate? I've spent almost every night here with you." I can't help the emotion that creeps into my voice, and Taylis turns and shifts to look at me directly.

"You are interested in me as a Chosen mate?"

"You? No! Of course not!" My skin flushed with heat and color, and I can only hope that I sat up quickly enough so he didn't see it.

"That is good."

His simple words felt like a knife to my heart. I wasn't even serious when I asked him. I was only curious about his stance on Chosen mates. At the time, none of my companions were Chosen, but I worried this was the direction they were headed. I didn't want to be left behind. Taylis was my best chance for a Chosen mate, and he shot me down so quickly it stung. But I couldn't forget the look in his eyes when I allowed that trace of vulnerability to creep into my voice. He looked interested. In me. In my words. Taylis never seems that way. For him, it's about pleasure. I please him. He pleases me. It's a good arrangement.

But in that moment of weakness, I considered what it would be like to want more.

"Yeah, it was just a thought," I said, hoping to smooth over this awkward conversation, so it's never brought up again. "A lot of females here are taking partners."

"Chosen mates," he clarifies. "They are desperate for mates. Any mates. And though I felt the same way for a time, I realized that a human female was not for me. They are too fragile. Weak." He returned his gaze to the ceiling. "I need a female who is equal to me."

My eyes widened. "If you wanted a female who was your equal, why did you leave Sidetha? Why would you choose exile?"

He didn't answer me. That was always Taylis' way. It still is.

When the conversation gets tough, the Taylis gets going. In his mind, anyway.

"If you want to Choose a mate, Alaska, please know I will not stop you."

Another shot to the heart. I didn't like how his words hurt me. Embarrassment flickered across my face, and I stood quickly. For the first time in years, my eyes felt hot and prickly. My heart painfully thudded against my chest. But Taylis didn't get up. Didn't even move. Just kept staring at the ceiling. I hated how he never looked me in the eye when he had a real conversation. And by Taylis' standards, anything beyond food talk qualified as real. I resisted the urge to snap something that would sting because it wouldn't have done any good.

I like to think of myself as numb. But Taylis warms up a part of my body that I think would be best left alone.

I BLINK AGAIN, FIGHTING THE RUSH OF EMOTIONS THAT SURGES through with this memory. I still remember how I thought about going to Arizona and telling her that Taylis' words bothered me. But I couldn't. She doesn't think anything bothers me. That's why she orders me around, gives me the toughest clients — the cruelest ones. I'm cold as ice Alaska. She doesn't need to hear about how a client's words hurt my little feelings. Gathering myself and dusting off my skirt, I decide to head back to the lairs. But I realize I'm not alone. Taylis stands only a few feet in front of me, head cocked to the side, a frown etched on his face. I'm feeling vulnerable after just reliving a painful memory about him, and I try to push away the urge to rush up to him and bury myself in his toned, bulky arms like I'd seen Taya do not too long ago.

"What are you doing out this far? Alone?" He glances around as though expecting something to jump out at him. "You are alone, yes?"

I don't like what he's insinuating. Does he think I came out here with one of his brothers for a quick lay? To come all this way to make sure I wasn't caught? After all this time, I guess he still views me as rent-a-sex, and I resist the urge to sneer. "I'm alone."

"You shouldn't be."

"It's still light out," I say, not in the mood to be reprimanded like a child. "I was heading back to the lairs right now if you would have just given me a chance to get the words out."

He crouches down, lowering himself to my level. I'm not short by any means, but Taylis is all but seven feet tall. I'm still feeling vulnerable, but I'm doing my best to make sure he doesn't know that.

"Are you saying you came out here to check on me? How thoughtful of you."

He frowns, not saying anything.

I can't believe I didn't hear him coming. It's light out, so it's not like he could have blended in with the shadows. I should have at least heard his steps, but of course, Taylis caught me in a vulnerable position. Again. His silence alone is making me uncomfortable, so I do my best to stare right back. His dark hair hangs directly over his yellow eyes, a constant reminder that he needs a trim. It's longer in the front than it is in the back, but maybe that's for the best because everything about Taylis' face is sullen. Grumpy. Even now, knowing he came all the way out here to check on me, he looks as though it was nothing more than an inconvenience. His full lips are pulled down into a deep frown, and his large jaw is tilted downward, even though he's below my eye level. Even crouched down, he makes me feel small and delicate.

Fragile is the word he likes to use when describing humans.

He probably thinks I look fragile right now.

"Well, now that you know I'm alive and not fucking any of your brothers on the sly, I guess you can go now." He frowns, still no answer, golden eyes locked on mine. There's disappointment written on his harsh features. But why? Is he disappointed he had to come out here? Disappointed he didn't catch me in the act of fucking one of his brothers? I swallow hard. Or is he disappointed because I'm *not* fucking someone else so he can finally have a reason to leave me? "Unless you expect me to walk back with you?"

He rises back to his full height, and I wince, confused about what he's going to do next. I'm not a Sidyth; I can't sniff out his damn emotions by slicking my tongue across my lips.

But I can see that he's pitched a significant tent in his shorts. *What the hell?*

So that's why he came. He got horny and wondered where his sex toy went.

The image makes me frown, even when Taylis advances quickly enough that I back myself into the trunk of the nearest tree. He stares down, breathing hard, eyes darting back and forth.

"If you want to fuck me, do it already. I'm not down for all this foreplay." I'm trying my best to sound nonchalant, but I'm sure Taylis can see how hard my heart is pounding against my chest.

He traces his fingers over my sternum and around the scoop of my tank, not quite touching my breasts, but making me shiver just the same. My body is giving in to him. Wanting him. I hate that. Even after all this time and listening to Taylis say that he doesn't want me for anything but sex, I'm turned on by his touch. I've never allowed myself to enjoy the touch of a male. Honestly, there was never that much to enjoy. But Taylis' touch is different. I throw my head back as his body lowers, shadowing mine.

"Tell me next time you want to go beyond the borders," he growls.

"Why? Because you'd lose your little sex toy?"

He snarls, pulling his body away from mine. For such a brief moment, there's a flicker of hurt on his sharp features. *Did my words bother him? Was he hurt by what I said? Is it possible that I'm more than a sex toy for him?* The thought shouldn't make me excited. I reach forward, but he snaps his body away from mine as though I'm a slimy Octonod. My hand freezes over the air between us only for a moment before it numbly drops back down to my side.

"That's it, isn't it?" I ask, growing hard and angry with his strange hot and cold behavior. "You're hot and horny, and you couldn't find your walking, talking blow job device?"

His expression shifts to fury, and his hands curl into fists, and scales splay away from his skin as though trying to get away from his anger. I don't think I've ever seen him this angry. And I'm still not entirely sure what his problem is. Is he mad that I called him out? Pointed out and reminded him that he doesn't think of me as a possible mate but a decent enough blow-up doll? I stare up at him, daring to say anything, but his expression only remains furious. If we weren't so far away from the lairs, I would run, but I'm afraid of heading in the wrong direction. I don't want whatever happened to Arizona to happen to me. I need to be smarter than her in more ways than one.

"What do you want, Taylis?" I hiss, annoyed with his silence. "If you want to fuck me, fuck me. If you want me to walk back with you, say so. But say what you want—" the words get caught in my throat as he storms back up to me. His face no longer looks as angry, but he's still damn intimidating when he looms over me. I fight the urge to run. But oh God, how I want to run. Not only because he frustrates me but because I like that he's so frustrating. "What do you want, Taylis?"

"I don't know." His voice comes out raspy and harsh, barely reaching my ears. I hear the words, but I don't know what they mean. I can guess because Taylis reaches out and grabs both my wrists and holds them over my head. His hand descends below my skirt.

"What are you doing?" I rasp anyway. "You said you didn't know what you want."

"I want you," he says thickly, pushing his fingers through the folds of my cunt and making me cry out, all miscommunication cut off for the time being.

CHAPTER 3

TAYLIS

I've lost it again.

I have lost my senses when it comes to that infuriatingly icy, human, Alaska. I shouldn't have allowed myself to touch her. Things always end up bad when I'm not able to resist her. Even now, raising from my bed, she's ready to run. I should tell her to do it. To find someone. A worthy mate. She wants one, even if she'd never admitted that to herself. I can sense the change in her scent. Now that her female companion, Arizona, has taken Drozass for a mate, she looks at me differently.

I cannot tell if she wants me for a mate because she wants me, or because Arizona has a mate of her own.

I should not care either way, but when Alaska stands and heads towards my lair opening, I fight back the urge to call her back. I know she will listen to me. Ever since I learned more about her history, I found out that she does well with orders. Arizona tells her what to do. There is a dark history that Alaska will not tell me about. That is fine. I shouldn't want to know. She is human. She is fragile. Taking her as a mate would only end up being a problem for both of us.

And so, despite the calling in my hearts, I let her go.

She doesn't look back.

I sit up from the bed once I am alone and reach for the nearest pair of shorts. I'm still nude from the night before so the shorts feel snug against my throbbing cock, and I probably should have asked Alaska to do something about it before she ran off this suns rising. She would have done so. But that's what makes the situation with Alaska even more troubling. She wouldn't say no. She would never deny me anything. Looking back on our time together, I used to think it was marvelous that she would not fight or argue with me. So many of the females are difficult despite their lack of strength and size. They expect favors from my brothers. But that's not how Alaska functions.

"That female infuriates me," I growl under my breath, about to push the curtain aside.

"Still?" The voice questioning me stands right outside my lair opening, and I resist the urge to snarl. Drozass stands before me, hair disheveled, but grinning. His very expression makes me defensive because I understand the cause of it.

"Did you see where she went? What direction?" I look up and down the halls, trying to catch Alaska's scent, but it's already faded in the musky air of the underground lairs. Drozass doesn't say anything at first, and I slowly lift my head. He's still smiling at me. "Brother. I am not in the mood. I want to know if she's doing anything stupid—"

"Your mate is a problem," he says crisply, shaking his head. "After what happened to my Arizona—"

"Alaska doesn't know what happened to your mate," I hiss. "That is not my problem. Was Alaska heading towards the main opening or not?"

I storm towards the central lair opening when Drozass doesn't respond, and he falls in line right beside me, easily matching my stride. I know he's trying not to upset me, but his Chosen mate and my pleasure mate are companions. And yet, for some reason, Alaska does not wish to see Drozass' mate. It shouldn't bother me. I shouldn't care, but Alaska has always been so withdrawn. This is the first time I've seen her take a stand against anything or anyone. I'm curious about what could have caused the change.

When Alaska's scent grows stronger, I become less worried. Perhaps, she has gone to speak to some of the other females. The short one with yellow hair. The tall one with spots of dirt upon her pale face. Alaska still seems to have no problem speaking with them, so maybe she is growing more social once again.

Which means that she would spend less time with me.

I am not sure I like the idea of that.

"If your female does not listen to mine, I will tell you what happened in the strictest of confidence," Drozass says, dropping his voice to a low whisper. "Come. Let us get something to eat."

Despite my trepidation of losing track of Alaska, I follow Drozass because I am still trying to convince myself that she does not matter. Drozass places a stale slice of banbask into my hand and crosses his arms across his chest. "Well, speak, brother," I say. "Are you going to take all day?"

He shakes his head. "Chocal is gone."

"Yes. I know that."

"He tried giving Arizona to the *outsiders.*"

My expression shifts wildly. His words have caught me off guard, but instead of the proper reaction, I grow stony. "What did Arizona do to him?"

Drozass hisses. "You know she did nothing. Chocal was always the problem. He tricked my mate into thinking she had a confidant because your female would not speak to her. If you could get your female under control, then instances like this would not be a problem."

"She is not my female."

"You give her pleasure, yes? She gives you pleasure?"

"That does not make her my responsibility."

Drozass polishes off his piece of banbask and dusts off his hands while shaking his head. I can feel the disappointment radiating from his skin, but I don't point it out. Not only is Drozass younger than me, but he is also lothid; poor. His words should mean nothing to me — less than nothing. But I still am stung when he begins to move past me.

"You should think about what you are doing with that one," he says in a gentle reminder. "The females are here now, but they are not all guaranteed to stay."

"I don't want a mate," I hiss.

Drozass' eyes widen. "Don't want a mate? Or you don't want to disappoint the very family who sent you away by taking an alien as a mate?"

Scales splay away from my skin. "You don't know anything, *lothid*." I have gone too far. Such terms are not supposed to hold any value on Hethdiss. Tothids. Mithids. Lothids. All the various social standings are not valid here. No matter how much credits we had back on the fatherland, they do no good on Hethdiss. Drozass is my equal unless we return to Sidetha, and he has no plans to. Most of my brothers feel the same as him, knowing that our brothers on the fatherland will never accept aliens as official Chosen mates. I didn't care for what he insinuated though. And so I had to fight back.

Only, I think my words were inappropriate.

Quickly, I bow my head. "I am sorry, brother. That was wrong of me."

"Why? It is not a lie. I am lothid as you are a tothid. That is simply the ways things were. On Sidetha. But I do not know if you have noticed, but we are no longer on the fatherland. Here, we are equals. And if you wish to throw such words at me, the next time you do, I may not be so forgiving." He drops his voice to a low hiss, and I do my best not to back away. Drozass is a good fighter. He comes from low credits. He's fought for everything he's ever had. I know our fight would be entirely one-sided. "Do you understand me, Taylis? I understand you are frustrated with your female, but do not take it out on me."

"I already apologized," I remind him, lifting my head as a few of the females enter the space. They are the pleasure mates of Cade and Dash. The two others who are companions of Alaska's. Hoping to lighten the mood, I turn away from Drozass and fix my attention on them. "Is there an official gathering starting I have not been made aware of?"

The two females curl up the lips, saying nothing to me at first. I still feel Drozass staring at me, but I suppose the conversation is finished for now. I want him to challenge me for a moment. I would lose, but at least losing a sparring battle would give me something else to think about. I'm spending too much time thinking about Alaska and her female companions.

"You're always such an ass," the one with dirt specks on her face says to me, reaching into the nearest cabinet and grabbing a *taieta* bar. She takes a hearty bite, and the nasty scent perfumes the air. It is far too sweet, but the humans enjoy it, so I suppose I am not one to judge. "Say, have you seen Alaska? Is she in your room? I want to talk to her."

"No." I shake my head. "I do not know where she went, female."

"Kansas," she grumbles. "It's been a year. You know my name is Kansas."

"He knows. It's like you said, though. He's an ass."

My eyes widen as I feel Alaska enter the space, her scent immediately wafting over my nostrils and taking over my senses.

She glides in our direction, and though she doesn't stand close to me, she doesn't stand near the other females. She's a hand or two taller than the shorter one with yellow hair and a hand or less taller than the dirt faced one—err, Kansas. When I see her not wanting to stand near me, I must fight every urge in my body to pull her close.

"You're going to have to talk to her eventually, Alaska," the one called Kansas says to her, avoiding my gaze. "We all think it's time to chat."

"About what? The fact that you've all lost your minds?" my females grumbles. "I have nothing to say to her."

"You should at least speak to her about what happened in the woods with Chocal," the one with yellow hair says softly. "She won't say anything to us, but I think it was bad. She'll probably tell you, Alaska."

"If you make a damn effort," Kansas snaps.

"Don't talk to her like that," I find myself sneering at the female. Her light brown eyes widen, and her chin tilts to fix me with a frown.

"Back off, Taylis," Alaska says in a bored tone.

"I'm just saying," Kansas continues. "There's been a divide forming for over a year now, and if you don't fix it, Arizona is going to cut you out of her life completely. Is that what you want?"

She doesn't respond. I don't know much about Alaska's relationship with the females, but I know she views Arizona as a leader. Arizona gives her orders, and Alaska completes them. Makes me wonder if she ordered Alaska to pleasure me. Makes me very angry. I will have to speak to Alaska about this at some point – not that it would change anything.

"You don't know what I want." I catch Alaska's strained response to the female's question, and I'm surprised by the emotion that floods through her voice.

I'm not used to it. Alaska has always been a pain because she does not often show emotion, but when I see or hear flashes of it, there is nothing I enjoy more. The crack in her voice shoots straight to the tip of my cock, and I notice her lower her head.

"That is enough. *Come, Alaska.* Let us go the talas and—"

"She doesn't have to listen to you," Kansas says, though the look on her face is comical when Alaska saunters right up beside me. It is as I always thought. She cannot refuse me when I speak in a specific tone. She cannot deny me. And though it should be a powerful weapon to wield, part of me wishes that Alaska would fight me.

"I think that she does," I say in a low voice, daring to wrap my arm around Alaska's soft, toned shoulders. She doesn't lean into my touch, but I wouldn't expect that from her. I lower my chin, choosing to ignore the other females staring at me like I'm the one with the issues. "Would you like to go outside? The weather is pleasant."

"For nude bathing?" Kansas grumps.

"*Sun basking* is the appropriate term, but I was thinking of sitting in silence," I say in return, "something she cannot enjoy when either of you is around."

The dirt-faced one snaps back as though I have taken my hand to her. Not that I ever would. I may still be unsure about what to do with Alaska, but that does not mean I am like my brothers on the fatherland. I would never take a hand to a female even if she infuriated me more than the very female standing beside me. Though I think it would be impossible for a female to be more frustrating than her, anyway. Somehow, I've got to fight whatever confusion is blossoming in my hearts when I'm around her. She is an alien. She is drama free. She does not cause problems. I can enjoy her for now. But once we can return to the fatherland, I'll be on the first ship home.

I cannot allow myself to Choose an alien for a mate.

But if forced, I suppose Alaska would be the most obvious choice.

For a moment, I allow myself to indulge at the idea of having a mate, even an alien. Alaska is not unpleasant to look at, and I have seen plenty of the mixed-species sprogs. The skin would be a very light blue, and the hair would be dark. It would not be a terrible thing. And then I would see no reason to return to the fatherland. Back to the endless parties on the mountains with aliens dancing upon platters and doing whatever is asked of them because they have received credits. *No.* I would not have to return to any of that; rather, I couldn't return to any of that if I took an alien as a mate.

But for some reason, I still hesitate, even when I look down at the top of Alaska's head and carefully move her away from the chatty females. Let them chatter at their pleasure mates. My Alaska doesn't have to listen to them when I am around.

The weather is pleasant beyond the lairs, with no clouds hanging above, and the atmosphere is dry and hot. Without wasting another moment, I bend over to peel off my shorts, ignoring the squeak of surprise that comes from the female my brother Wixlass spends time with. As I sling my shorts over my shoulder, her eyes pinched shut, and once again, she has buried herself against Wix's chest. Strange. Does he not think she is weak? Doesn't her weakness bother him? Judging by his expression, I can see it does not, but I shake my head anyway, making sure Wix notices.

The fresh air feels incredible in my lungs, and I take a slow, deep breath once the stench of my brothers and their mates no longer fills my nose. I glance down at Alaska again, and though I can feel the curiosity in her scent, she follows me without question. She is a female. It takes strength to put so much trust in someone else. But I suppose it is also a weakness if the wrong male gets his hands on her.

I would be the right male. I would wield my power with care.

"I thought you were totally against going this far beyond the lairs," Alaska says, her tone cautious.

"I said it was dangerous if a female was alone. Stay close to me." I go to reach for her arm, but she pulls it away.

"I'm all right."

"Very well."

I lead her up a gentle rise in the ground and stare closely at the cluster of talas ahead of us — Dilewiler territory. Amazingly, Prince Korben felt so comfortable setting up the lairs so close to the wild beasts. But it seems, they are very territorial. Chentan informed me that dilewilers would not leave the shelter of the talas unless necessary. That is a good thing because in those woods are monsters who could easily rip alien flesh apart. I would be able to fight off a dilewiler or two, but a human female would be completely helpless to stop the attack.

But it is not the dilewilers that worries me.

No. After my brief conversation with Drozass, I suppose the beasts should be the least of my worries.

Chocal betrayed Prince Korben. The *outsiders* must now be aware that we are holding alien females in his territory. I can only imagine how curious this makes them. If they do not have the strength or willpower, I do not think they could be gentle with them. It has been too long without pleasure. I don't think I would be so much in control of myself had I not received pleasure on the regular because of Alaska. Oddly, I am a better male because of her complacency.

But I suppose none of that matters if an *outsider* were to grow curious about an unmated alien female. Because that is what Alaska is. Unmated. Even in exile, no male would dare steal a mated female. But the ones who do not have Chosen mates? They are the ones who are in the most danger. I believe this is a reason why Drozass broke down and accepted the brown-skinned female. Briefly, I consider if it would be a wise decision to Choose Alaska. To keep her safe. Only we would have to know, and it seems this is something Alaska wants, even if it's only to please her female companions.

"Do you wish to be Chosen mates?" I ask carefully.

Alaska stiffens, blinking up at me as though she were having night terrors. "What did you say?"

"I asked if you wanted to be Chosen mates. You and I."

"Is that why you brought me out here?"

I tilt my head to the side, wondering what the best response would be. I consider lying to her and saying I did, but I do not think Alaska would believe me. My question is coming out of nowhere to her, probably, and there is no reason to hide my intentions.

"There are unmated males," I explain, jutting my chin towards the dilewiler territory. "Those male Sidyths who did not want to stay with Prince Korben. Some have fled north. Others south. But there *are* others."

"How many?" Her question sounds forced. Bordering on dull.

"I would imagine close to six," I respond in a low voice. "None of them have mates. But word is spreading that there are females here. Even if they are alien females."

She winces slightly. "So, that is why you wish to be Chosen mates? Because of them?"

I nod. "If you and I are mated, they would not dare take you away."

"Why?"

"Because when our mates are in danger, we have been known to go into a rage. We care that much about the female we Choose."

"But we wouldn't be real mates," she says. "I'd be your mate in name only. There's no reason for them to worry about going in a rage. Because you wouldn't care."

I hiss under my breath. "I would care."

"I mean, officially." She takes a step away from me, beginning to pace. "If you are worried about other Sidyths taking me or, whatever, Choosing me as a mate won't do anything. They wouldn't have to fear you going into a rage. Because we wouldn't be real mates, right?"

"Yes, but…" I trail off, unsure how I wish to proceed.

Alaska's response to my request to be Chosen mates isn't what I expected. I think she is interested in having me as a mate, so why is she fighting? Why not just say yes and move on? And while yes, she is probably right that her kidnapping would not put me into an official rage, I would care. I would be angry. Furious. Just thinking about another male touching her… one with no honor or shame… I curl my hands into fists, pressing my claws into my palms to settle down. I shouldn't take Alaska's reasoning so personally. She's only doing what she does best — being logical. Cool. Cold. Almost icy. But just as soon as I'm about to take back my suggestion, Alaska uncrosses her arms.

"Let's do it, then."

My eyes widen, and Alaska has stopped right in front of me. I can't quite get a read on her emotions suddenly, and this frustrates me much. I've always been able to taste her feelings in the air either through my nose or tongue, but now I feel nothing. Not anger. Sadness. Disappointment. Not even joy or relief. I taste nothing. For some reason, I'm bothered by this lack of anything. I should be used to this with Alaska, but after agreeing to be Chosen mates? Shouldn't there be something? Some bond? Pleasure? A shared smile of some sort?

"Alaska. Did you hear what I said?" I try once more, hoping that perhaps she misunderstood what I offered. "I said we should be Chosen mates. For your safety."

She nods. "Yes. I understand. We would be mates in name only. It wouldn't be the real deal. And though I don't think it would make much of a difference because even if I were taken, it wouldn't bother you—"

"*Stop saying that.*"

She blinks. "Saying what?"

"Saying I wouldn't care if you were taken. Stop. Just because we are not real Chosen mates does not mean I do not care about you. You are weak. Fragile. I want to protect you because we have been pleasure mates for a long time now." I grind my teeth together, fighting my frustration. "I Choose you."

"Unofficially—"

"I Choose you," I repeat, fighting every urge in my body demanding that I scream to hold her attention. "As far as anyone will know, we are Chosen mates. We will speak to Prince Korben, and it will be known throughout the lairs that you and I are mates."

She blinks up at me a second time, her expression still dull and empty as anything. I want her to say something. Anything to remind me she has some emotion or passion brewing behind those cold, blue eyes. Isn't she going to fight me? Argue that this is a farce? A fake arrangement? Why do I care? Why do I want her to fight to make this real?

There must be a way to ignite the idle passion lurking beneath.

"As my Chosen mate, you will be by my side unless I instruct otherwise. It will be for your safety. You are *not* to go beyond the borders unless you are with me. Not with another male. Only me. And if you are having problems dealing with your female companions, I want you to find me. Only me. Do you understand?"

"You and only you," she says blandly, making my scales splay.

"Do you have a problem? I thought you wanted this—"

"The question was hypothetical. Don't flatter yourself and

think I want you to Choose me. I know it wouldn't mean anything. But if this is the best way to keep me safe and preventing what happened to Arizona, I'll go along with it. I probably wouldn't be able to stand another one of you big guys anyway."

I take in a deep, trembling breath. I'm making a fool of myself for a female who doesn't want me. For a female I don't even want! But for whatever reason, I can't take the words back. I frown down at her. "Are you truly going to be all right with this? We will be the only ones who know we are Chosen mates in name only."

"I don't have a problem with it." Slowly, her eyes lift to mine, and finally, I see something flicker — some emotion. I'm not even sure what. "Did you want to consummate our Chosen marriage now? That's what the others do, right?"

"Are you aroused?" I ask, taking a step closer and cupping her mound without hesitation. She gasps under my touch but doesn't move away. The curls covering her slit are damp, and I can't stop the one side of my mouth from curling up in the corner. *Despite her words, she wants this.* "You are aroused."

"Am I?" Her eyes dip down to where I'm holding her, before flicking back to mine. "You gonna do something about it?"

"Do you want me to?"

"Do *you* want to?"

I fight the urge to hiss once again, but I cannot deny myself. I suppose it makes sense. Even if in name only, this female is mine. She belongs to me, and it is part of my obligation to take care of her. I push several of my fingers through her folds, gathering her sweet honey that collects and gently pull my hand away from her skirt. My claws and fingertips glisten under the suns, and I stare hard at the female before me. I shouldn't indulge myself. Shouldn't so easily allow her to win. She's not going to fight me, so why not take what I want? We're only going to hurt ourselves with this little arrangement, but I still lift my fingers to my lips and lick off the juices.

Alaska swallows hard but remains aloof. If I weren't used to looking so closely at her for such a long time, I wouldn't have even noticed. But I know her. I recognize the movement of her throat muscles.

"Do you want some?" I ask in a low voice, pushing my still glistening fingers towards her face. "If you will not admit how you feel, then perhaps you should taste yourself and learn the truth."

She pushes my hand away. "My question was hypothetical. It always was."

"You never wanted a mate? Not any mate?"

I lower my hand, feeling the moment shatter as her lips remain pressed together. My cock is crying out for some much-needed attention, but I won't ask Alaska to take care of it because she would. Even if she did not want to, she would do it because I asked. One command from me, and she's like wet sand in my palms. I can mold her however I see fit. And though I'm aching to take advantage of that power, the words will not come.

And apparently, neither will I.

"What if my question were not hypothetical?" I try next, hoping to shock her. I want to see that flicker of emotion cross her face again, even if it's only for the briefest of moments. "What if I wanted you to Choose me as a mate officially?"

"I would ask if that's what you wanted."

"And if I did want it?" I ask, leaning closer. "What would your answer be then?" I'm practically brushing my lips against her hair, but she doesn't move away.

"My answer would be whatever you wanted it to be."

"Even if you did not want me?"

"Even if I did not want you," she says, lifting her chin to meet my eyes.

I hate that. It's the worst answer I could hear, but Alaska doesn't seem to regret it. Worse, I don't think she understands why there should be any reason to regret it. "Let me understand. Even if you did not want me as a mate, you would say yes if I asked?"

"If that's what you wanted."

"Even if you did not want me. Say it."

"Even if I did not want you."

I pull away, feeling a strange, painful emotion erupting in my chest. "I see. Well, then. Luckily for you, the question was only hypothetical."

"Are we still on, though? We're still mates?"

"Unofficial Chosen mates," I hiss. "Yes. Let us return to the lairs and request an audience with Prince Korben. If you have any questions for me about this arrangement, please speak now. I'm assuming that this information will be between us, yes? You don't wish to share this with any of your female companions?"

There it is again — the flicker of emotion passing through her calm, blue eyes.

"Alaska?"

"No. There is no one else I will tell. This arrangement and all the details will be just between us."

My shoulders slump without permission. "Very well. From this point on, we are Chosen mates."

From the looks on my brothers' faces, even though this isn't a typical arrangement, I expected there to be more excitement buzzing in the air. I thought Alaska would be pleased. As it is though, she merely turns and walks in the direction of the central lair. I'm not exactly sure what I could have done to make things turn out any differently, but for some reason, I am frustrated. Perhaps I should have lied to her and said this was official. Would I have seen a flicker of emotion then? Would she have smiled? Laughed? Thrown her arms around my neck and kissed me passionately? I try not to focus on it for too long. It shouldn't even matter.

Alaska will be my Chosen mate in the eyes of everyone at the lairs, and any *outsiders* will smell me all over her if they ever attempted to take her away. It's a good thing. It must be. This decision will keep Alaska safe, and she will receive praise from her female companions. Everything works out for the best for both of us.

So why do I feel empty? Why do I find myself wanting more?

When the lairs finally come into view, and we're about to cross into the clearing, I find myself reaching for Alaska's arm. This can't be it. It must be more than this. I must mean more to her than this. I hate that she won't give me more. I deserve more. Even if I don't want her to be my mate officially, I deserve more. I should get something that others have not seen.

Her passion. Her warmth.

Alaska spins in my direction; her expression neither happy nor sad.

And though the questions bubble on my tongue, when she looks at me like this, I can't bring any words to the surface other than, "Apologies. I thought a branch was about to swing in your face."

She looks at me as though I have lost my senses.

Perhaps I have.

Because suddenly, I find myself wanting more from Alaska.

I find myself also… wanting her.

CHAPTER 4

ALASKA

WHAT THE FLIPPING FANNY-PACK HAVE I DONE NOW?

I pull my knees closer to my chest in bed, staring down at the massive sleeping alien beside me, and try to figure out just what the hell is wrong with me. When did I become this person? I don't mind not showing my emotions, but now I'm giving myself to an alien who doesn't merely want pleasure, but a relationship. *A fake relationship*, but still. I should have told him no. I should have told him it was a bad idea and we'd both only get hurt.

Making sure to keep quiet, I throw my legs carefully over the side of the bed, and look back, making sure Taylis isn't waking up. He's snoring softly, the tip of his forked tongue peeking out from between his full, cerulean lips. I shouldn't even think about how pretty his mouth is. He's an alien. Not to mention a client. And while, yes, *technically* he's my Chosen mate, I don't mean that much to him.

Well, I guess I mean enough that he wants to keep me from being kidnapped.

Which I can only assume is what happened to Arizona and why Taylis is so worried about it.

Chocal kidnapped Arizona. He tried selling her off.

Now I feel like a piece of shit for not talking to her about it.

For the first time in almost ten days, I need to see her and talk to her. I quietly pull on my skirt and settle the flimsy fabric on my hips, wishing it were longer. But unfortunately, the taller you are, the less coverage you get from the star hussy skirts. Could be worse. Sloane can't even bend over in hers without giving everyone around her a pussy lips production.

After checking one last time that I haven't woken up Taylis, I sneak away from his lair and into the hallways. I'm honestly still processing what happened last night. And that's beyond the idea of being Chosen mates with Taylis. Chocal betrayed Arizona. Was he the one who hurt her? Was he the reason Arizona winces when she laughs or walks? Did he do that to her wrist? I shouldn't get so riled up, but just the idea of someone hurting her... my legs power forward and into the direction of her shared lair with Drozass.

After a quick pat on the curtain and Drozass inviting me inside, I see the look of shock on Arizona's face when our eyes meet. She's sprawled out on the bed, and immediately sits up straighter. "Well, holy shit," she says, waving her hand at Drozass who wants to say something. Perhaps tell me to go to hell. I guess he'd be in his right. But he closes his lips after Arizona sends him a warning glare to match her hand. "You're the last person I expected to see this morning."

"Did he hurt you?" I ask, not wanting to mince words. Drozass' eyes widen, and he takes a quick step towards me, but Arizona speaks first.

"Can you get some of that tea that makes me hyper?" she

says quickly, and Drozass spins in her direction. Her expression grows sickeningly sweet. "Please, baby? I could use a pick-me-up."

Confusion hits his features. "You need me to carry you?"

"It's an expression, baby. Please? Just some of the tea?"

Drozass eyes me. "Right now?"

She nods. "Right now."

Drozass' shoulders slack, but he doesn't argue. His movements are sharp when he maneuvers around me, but once he's gone, the tension leaves the room. I haven't spoken or checked in with Arizona in a long while, but now it suddenly feels as though no time at all has passed.

"Did he hurt you?" I ask.

"Hi and hello to you, as well."

"Did he hurt you?" I take a few shaky steps towards the end of the bed and rest my hands on the plush blanket. "Chocal. Did he—"

"What, you mean this?" She holds up her wrist, still bandaged. "No. Chocal didn't do that."

"And your other injuries? The one that makes you wince?"

"This?" She pulls up her shirt, revealing some healed bruises. They're faded but take up most of her torso. She lets the fabric fall. "No. Chocal didn't do that either."

"Then what?"

"It was the rodur."

I blink. "The... what?"

"Rodur." Her expression darkens. "They're like lizard gorillas. Big. They thought I was a sick baby or something."

"They hurt you?"

She shakes her head. "I don't think that was ever their intent. Well, I don't think that was ever her intent. There was one who..." she trails off, eyebrows pinching together at some implicit memory. She shakes her head. "Never mind. Long answer short? Chocal didn't do this. Just another one of the pleasant alien animals living in these woods around us."

I shudder to think what a lizard gorilla looks like and what kind of attention Arizona received to give her bruises like that. "But you're okay now? Drozass is taking care of you?"

Her expression shifts slightly. "He's doing what he can. But you know I've always been that chicks before dicks kind of girl."

"You had Dakota and Kansas," I say, feeling a surprising emotion wash over me. Guilt.

"I haven't told them what happened yet. Not all of it." She frowns. "And yeah, I had them. But I needed you, Alaska." She pats a spot next to her on the bed, and she must immediately see my nose scrunch up. "Sorry, babe, but sex smell is part of the job… even when it's not. Don't be a prissy. Sit down and talk to me." She pats the spot again, and I stroll over to the bed and pull down the blanket so I can sit on top of it rather than directly on the sheets. I may be a star hussy, but I don't exactly want to sit on sheets that have been freshly fucked on.

"I'm glad you finally decided to woman up and come talk to me," she says. "I've missed you. Even though you're a bitch, you're *my* bitch, and I missed you." She smiles, and it's the most beautiful look I've seen her wear in a long time. Happy, but not about Drozass. She's fucking happy about me. And for some reason, it hurts to think her happiness is genuine while mine is going to be a sham.

"I've missed you too," is all I can bring myself to say to her.

"I could tell," she says, laughing. "Especially when you'd run in the opposite direction every time you saw me coming. What was with that? Seriously. Is Taylis saying you can only spend time with him?"

I shake my head.

"Then what is it? Have I changed that much? I have a mate now. It's weird, and I get that. Fucking ridiculous. But whether you want to believe me or not, Alaska, I am happy. I like Drozass. I love him. Maybe once you have a mate—"

"I do have a mate."

She smiles. "Chosen mate is a little different than pleasure—"

"Taylis isn't a pleasure mate. Not anymore. He Chose me."

She looks skeptical. "When?"

"Last night. We talked about it. And it makes the most sense. He Chose me. I Chose him. We're officially mates now." I feel Arizona staring at me, probably trying to investigate my soul or something just as crazy sounding, and I have a hard time meeting her gaze. I know my face doesn't look like Arizona's. I'm not happy like she is. I'm not smiling. That's because though I have a Chosen mate, my relationship isn't real. My eyes start to prickle, and I quickly swipe at my face. "It stinks in here. The smell of Sidyth sperm is making me gag."

"I bet." Arizona's still looking at me, and she's got to know I'm changing the subject. "You and Taylis. Officially mated. Did you talk to Prince Korben?"

"Later today."

"And you wanted this?" I lift my chin, and I hate that doubt is written all over her exotic features. I quickly lower my head. "You don't want this. Ugh, Alaska. Did he order you to be his mate or something?"

"No," I say quickly, not wanting to paint Taylis in a harsh light. Technically, he hasn't done anything wrong. "That's not it. I told you. We talked about it. It makes sense."

"You don't love him." I feel her leaning closer. "*Alaska, you don't love him*. I can tell."

"I don't... I don't like the arrangement," I say thickly, fighting back tears I don't want to shed. Certainly not in front of Arizona. She probably can't even tell how hard I'm fighting. No one knows. To Arizona, I probably look like my cold, blasé self.

"Of course you don't," Arizona says. "Because you don't love him."

That's not it, I'm screaming at the top of my lungs in my head. I can't bring myself to meet her eyes. If I see the concern on her face as I hear it in her voice, I'm going to lose it. And I can't lose it. Arizona's been nothing but good to me. My alpha. My leader. My life. And yet, because of the way I am, she can't even tell what's bothering me. It has nothing to do with love. I only wish Taylis wasn't so clinical about everything. Sometimes I wish we were mates, but if we were, I'd want it to be real. I'd rather be true pleasure mates than fake Chosen mates.

Arizona tries reaching for one of my hands, and I snap away, standing from the bed and keeping my back to her. "I wanted you to know before anyone else," I say quickly. "Because you're my... you're the leader and all. I thought it made the most sense to tell you first."

"Is that the only reason you stopped by?"

I grimace. "And to... apologize. For not coming by sooner. Arizona, I had no idea what happened—"

"You never asked," she says, smiling. Like I'm acting exactly the way she always expects me to. "Look, I'm not mad, okay? I know you... must do things your way, all right? I'm honestly just happy you finally stopped by to speak to me. And I... uh... I guess congratulations are in order. You and Taylis are official mates." She lowers her voice. "Unless... do you want me to put a stop to it?"

I shake my head once more. "I'll figure it out on my own."

"I see. Wow."

I spin towards her. "What?"

"You've changed. Usually, you like me to figure things out for you. Now you're saying you're going to handle it on your own? Not to sound creepy, but I kind of always hoped you'd get to this point, but now that it's happening, I'm not sure I like it." She laughs again, but it's a fake sound to my ears. She's genuinely not happy to see me needing her less and less.

"I still need you," I admit in a low voice. "I always will." I bend down and reach across the bed and snatch her hand, squeezing it gently. "I still need you too, you know."

Her face softens. "Thank God."

A genuine smile hits my face. "Honestly, it makes the most sense, Arizona. Taylis told me about females needing mates to stay safe—"

"No, I get it," she says quickly. "If you're mated, even an *outsider* wouldn't try to take you."

"What Taylis is saying makes sense. I just wish …" I trail off, my eyebrows knitting together in deep thought. *What do I want? I'm used to feeling empty, but why does it bother me to feel this way now?*

"You wished you loved him," Arizona finishes.

I remove my hand. God, she doesn't understand me. No one does. And I have no one to blame but myself. "Maybe I wished he loved me."

Arizona's dark eyes widen, but she doesn't say anything. Not at first. Slowly, I lift my head to meet her eyes, and I can tell that she's processing.

"I should go—"

"You're not going anywhere." Her voice is sharper than usual, and though every fiber in my body is trying to rebel, I can't ignore an order from her. I sit up straighter though, meeting her hard expression right on. "Wow," she breaths. "You have changed."

"I'm the same person I always was, Arizona."

She shakes her head. "No. You're different. Is he the reason you're trying to stand on your own?"

"No."

"Then, why? What are you trying to prove?"

"I'm not trying to prove anything! All right? Everything I've ever known and been told for my entire life is now meaningless. Can we just say I'm having an identity crisis? Stop trying to turn this into something deep and dark. Maybe I only realized I can't depend on you anymore."

Arizona sucks in a breath. I consider taking my words back, but the moment my lips part, Arizona holds up a hand. "No. Don't go back on it. That's the ballsiest, most passionate thing I've ever heard you say in my life. Don't you dare take it back." The corner of her mouth curls up into a smile, but it doesn't quite meet her eyes. "I always kind of wondered what this moment would be like."

"What?"

"You realizing I'm not as great of a leader as you want me to be."

I wince. "It's not that."

She chuckles slightly. "That's what it is. For years, you've taken my word as gospel. It was nice at first. When we were all still building our reputation as the State Girls, if there was anyone I could count on more than myself, it was you. And I didn't understand it. I mean, I picked you, but you didn't even fight me. You did everything I asked." She shakes her head, pushing a hand through her dark waves. "I didn't want to ask questions. I guess I just really wanted to believe that I had some leadership qualities, you know?"

"You did," I say softly, wishing that I sounded more convincing.

Because Arizona *did* have leadership qualities, she still does. At least, she would if she wasn't trying to get knocked up an alien client on the promise she'll get to keep her mate and raise her baby.

"Say, you want to go for a walk?" Arizona asks, wincing as she rises to a standing position.

Instinct takes over, and I'm immediately by her side, making sure she's all right. She not-so-gently pushes me aside.

"I'm all right," she mutters. "Come on. I want to show you something."

My eyes widen. "Won't Drozass wonder where you went?"

She smirks. "Yes. I imagine he'll wonder."

I can't help returning her statement with a smile.

It doesn't take too terribly long before Arizona and I have left the secondary lair. A few Sidyths glance our way, but no one messes with Arizona. I guess I'm part of the package, but that's all right too. I'm enjoying spending time with my leader once again, err, or I think, maybe I should start referring to her as my friend. She hasn't said anything official, but it feels like the State Girls are already a whisper of the past.

Once Arizona has a spot picked right on the edge of the boundary, she takes a seat and pats the grass beside her. Still unsure about what this is all about, I take a seat. A small part of me will always want to follow her orders because I still view her as my leader. But another part of me wants to listen because I think it's the only way I'll be set free from the binds I've tied to her.

"It wasn't too much further than here," Arizona says, frowning in the direction of some large trees with dark purple trunks and lavender leaves. I hear the unmistakable sounds of alien animals in the distance, but if Arizona isn't worried about them, I'll try to keep my nerves calm. "Chocal brought me out here. Said he was taking me to the hot springs. But…"

She trails off, and I try to bite back the feeling of disappointment in this part of the story. Arizona knows better. She should have never gone off with a random male who wasn't her client. She'd grown soft. She'd grown to trust the Sidyths entirely too much. That was her downfall. Still, I bite back the words as she sighs and continues.

"You know. I never actually got to see an *outsider*. Isn't that weird? It never got that bad."

My eyes widen. "Wait. I thought Drozass said you were kidnapped with the intent to be—"

"Used as a bargaining tool," Arizona fills in. "Yeah. I guess Chocal got into some trouble with the *outsiders* and thought offering them an unmated female would put him back in their good graces. And it almost worked! That's the scary thing. I heard their voices." Her chin lifts slightly. "They sound different than a lot of the guys around here."

"How do they sound?"

Her eyebrows pinch together. "More... feral, I guess? Gruffer? Less concerned with refinement. Their voices still translated into my earpiece, but their accents were harsher. Sharper."

"Wait. So if outsiders didn't kidnap you, what happened?" My eyes lower to her wounds, even though they're tucked away under her top.

She takes in a deep, trembling sigh. "I haven't told anyone about what happened other than Drozass."

"Not Kansas or Dakota?"

"Especially not them." She frowns, turning in my direction, "You're the only one I trust with this information, Alaska."

"Why?" I ask, hating how touched I am.

"I know you can keep a secret." I suck in a gasp. "You've never told anyone about what happened to you back on Earth. Other than to me and that's only because I ordered you. That's why I trust you with what I'm about to say. You're trustworthy, Alaska. You're a good person. I know me and the girls crack jokes about you being a robot, but that's only because Kansas and Dakota don't know you like I do. They don't know how strong and human you are."

"So what?" I ask, trying to keep my voice steady. "You trying to say... what are you trying to say to me, Arizona?"

"I'm saying I'm not fit to be your leader any longer. This place broke me down, Alaska. Some ways were good. Some ways bad. The point is, you're right. You shouldn't turn to me as a leader any longer. What happened to me here, in the woods, with Chocal, and with Drozass, changed me. I'm not Arizona – leader of the State Girls. I'm just a woman. An ordinary woman who's found a small piece of happiness. And I want you to do the same."

"With Taylis?"

"With whoever or whatever you want," she says in a low voice. "If you have feelings for him, do something about it. Or don't. And if you don't have feelings for him, do something about it. Or don't. The point is, I'm not going to tell you what to do. I want you to figure out on your own. I know you're scared of making your own decisions and would rather be led. But if that's still something you need; I can't give it to you. If you're not ready to lead yourself, then maybe you should let someone else lead you for a little while and go from there."

"Taylis," I repeat, lowering my head.

"Only if you want him," she reminds me, sliding closer across the grass and resting a palm on my knee. "I'm just saying it's your call now. All of it is your call. I can't do it anymore. I can't in good conscience tell you what to do anymore. Any of you."

My chin lifts, and I gaze out through the thick trees before fixing my attention back on Arizona. "Seriously, what the fuck happened to you out there? If you didn't see any *outsiders*, then what?"

She doesn't answer me again. "If you're worried about depending on Taylis, you could tell him about your past. See how it goes from there," she says instead, her words causing me to flinch back.

"What the hell?" I grumble. "No. We're not talking about me."

Arizona shrugs. "Something to think about. But if you want to know what happened to me, sit back and get your popcorn ready."

"We don't have any popcorn," I say drily.

"Then I guess just hold on to your titties because this story is about to get nasty."

Her expression shifts to something more severe despite her words, and though I want to push her, I won't. Arizona may have renounced herself as my leader, but I'll still respect her as a friend. She saved me. She saved all of us. Washington, myself, Dakota, and even Kansas. She's owed our respect for the rest of our lives.

Which is why her suggestion about telling Taylis about my past remains on my mind, even as Arizona speaks about her pretty disgusting and horrific experience.

CHAPTER 5

TAYLIS

THERE IS SOMETHING STRANGE GOING ON WITH MY PLEASURE mate. Ugh, I mean my Chosen mate. I am still having difficulty adjusting to the change, even if it is only verbal. Drozass informed me that Alaska spoke with his mate, and honestly, she hasn't been the same since. Alaska appears more shaken. She doesn't eat much, and though I cannot hear her words, I know she is muttering to herself. I am only able to catch mere fragments.

That's why I'm curious if something is wrong with her.

It was only a few hands of time later after her returning from her conversation with Arizona that I noticed her change in behavior. She slept in my bed but tossed and turned about and thrashed her arms in the air. This never happened before, and it was quite alarming to observe the first time.

Mainly because even when I awakened Alaska, she pretended everything was fine.

She acted as though I lost my senses and not her.

I tried speaking to several of my brothers about the matter, but they seemed to believe this to be an 'alien issue.' A female alien issue, more accurately and to not pay much attention to it. But I paid attention. And the closer attention I paid, the more I worried Alaska's conversation with Arizona was to blame for the change.

"Chentan, please," I begged our alien specialist after several passings of this strange behavior. "You must know what could be wrong with her."

He shrugged. "Perhaps she is anxious. Aliens have much on their minds. Have you spoken to her about the matter?"

"Of course," I hiss. "But she denies it. She always denies it!"

"Perhaps she wants a sprog?"

"Ugh. No. If you understood her, you would know this is not the case."

"Then what does she mutter?" he asks inquisitively. "When she thrashes about? Does she say anything in particular? Anything that would give you reason to worry?"

I frown down at him. "Alien names, I believe. From her homeworld, I suppose."

"Then perhaps she is merely homesick?" Chentan guesses, shrugging. "Most of these females have had a traumatic experience. Many of them have only known cruelty in their lives. I know this situation is strange for many of them."

"She's been here for over a year," I grumble. "Why would she think about things that cannot be changed?"

"I don't know, Taylis. That's up to you to find out. She is your mate, after all. If you are noticing changes in behavior, why not simply ask her about it?"

"I have," I snarl in reminder.

"Ask her again. Again, and again. Never let her think for a moment that her suffering is not at the forefront of your mind, brother. Perhaps then, she may be more comfortable speaking to you about what bothers her. Next time she has night terrors, listen to her words. Is she saying a name? If so, what? Remember that name. Ask her about it. If she blows you off, ask her again."

"Then what? What if she grows angry with me?"

"She *will* grow angry with you. Get past that anger. Beneath her anger is something much more painful. Perhaps the kindness she has been shown forces her to reflect on the cruelty she's suffered at the hands of others. Prince Korben told me several of the females have difficult backgrounds. Probably more than you or I could imagine."

"I don't know…"

"Has anything changed recently for your mate?"

The conversation with Arizona. Alaska still has not told me what they spoke about.

"No," I lie, hating how bitter the words taste in my mouth. "Yes. But she will not speak to me about that either." I lean closer to Chentan. "Do you think I should continue to question even if it angers her?"

"If she's this angry about questions, then I'm guessing it's because the answers bring her pain."

My hearts ache at the idea of Alaska suffering and not feeling comfortable enough to talk to me about it. Yes, we are Chosen mates in name only, but before that, we were genuine pleasure mates. Some part of me still wants to believe Alaska and I have some connection despite both of us being calm and professional. But it seems I am wrong. I misjudged her, more importantly, I underestimated how much she was able to keep inside.

"I'm afraid I can't stay longer," Chentan says in a low voice, slapping a palm across his broad chest. "Glykoran wished to speak to me about his mate."

"Oh? Anything wrong?"

"I'm honestly not sure," he says vaguely, spinning away and speaking over his shoulder. "I know he and his mate are trying to have a sprog, but other than that, I'm not sure what else it would be about. If you have any further questions concerning your mate, feel free—"

"I can handle it from here," I say shortly, happy to see my brother go.

Because now it gives me a chance to see what my mate is up to.

Exiting the lairs, I'm hardly surprised when I see her in the distance. Alone. Always alone. Her back is to the sanctuaries, but I notice her small hands closing and opening, repeatedly. I recognize this as something she does when she is feeling on edge, but for the life of me, I don't have the slightest idea about what's upsetting her so much.

The conversation with Arizona. The names she calls. They must be names because I don't recognize the words. They do not translate.

Who are these people she calls out to in the middle of the night? What have they done to Alaska to make her thrash about and scream in terror? Why won't she tell me about any of it? I thought being Chosen mates would allow her to open up to me more, but it seems she is more closed off than ever.

Realizing she doesn't notice my approach; I keep my steps soft and light across the fields in her direction. Perhaps, she will be less cautious about what she speaks of in private. Maybe I can understand the names she speaks of, why they upset her, and why she is so desperate to keep them a secret. Her murmurings fill my ears more and more as I draw closer, and the air smells intense with anxiety and worries. I steady myself behind the thick trunk of a tala and fall silent, hoping desperately that Alaska or any of my brothers will not notice me.

She paces now.

Her steps are almost as light and quick as mine between two large talas. I notice the sounds of dilewilers in the distance, but other than that, I sense nothing that would put my mate in danger. Both lairs are on high alert because of what happened with Chocal, but it seems this does not concern Alaska. She occasionally rests her palms on the trunks of the talas and pulls down a branch or two filled with *tuftas*. She plucks them off the branch one by one, throws the branch aside, only to begin pacing again.

But her movements tell me nothing. I'm waiting for her to speak. Say something that reminds me of her words when she's having night terrors. If something truly is painful to my mate, I need to know. I may be her Chosen mate by necessity but I am going to do everything a suitable mate is supposed to do. If she is hurt, I want to make it better. If someone has hurt her, I want to rip out their throat and toss it over the Great Cliff. I don't want Alaska ever to think I will not be faithful to my bond to her merely because of the circumstances. I will protect her. I will devote myself to her. I will make her feel safe and beautiful, and I will tend to her wounds if she needs me to.

The problem is, I'm not sure if she understands she needs me to.

She stops pacing, snaps a branch off a tala, performs the same act with the *tuftas*, throws the branch and begins again. I've never seen her do anything like this before. Not any female. Not even any alien. Not that I've paid much attention to the females, but this only further reminds me of how weak and fragile they are. If something in Alaska's past riles her up this much, I can only imagine how shattered she would be if something just as tragic happened in her present.

More importantly, I'm shocked by how much I would want to be there for her.

My hearts thump heavily against my chest as I continue to

observe my fragile, frightened human. My mind drifts, considering what would happen if I followed Chentan's advice, stormed up to her and demanded to know what was bothering her. Whatever it is, I'm sure I could fix it. I'm not the strongest male, but I am crafty. If she's upset with Chocal for what he did to her friend, I will track him down and put his head on a stake for her amusement. If she—

All thoughts of murder come to a grinding halt when Alaska sighs loudly and stops pacing. She glances around the talas, almost as though to check if she's alone and slumps against the nearest trunk. I shift carefully to see what she is doing, but her back is merely to the trunk, and her thighs are slowly spreading.

I swallow hard.

She parts her thighs further, and a hit of arousal nearly spars me in the nostrils. I long to cough from the exotic scent, but I don't want Alaska to know I'm here. She wants to make sure no one is around for what she's about to do. I bite down hard on my lower lip as her hand crawls down her stomach and gently brushes against the curls covering her slit. I almost lose it right then and there when a little mewl of a sound escapes her lips from that small little touch.

Scheita.

Unable to help myself, my hand seeks out my cock over top of my shorts, and I rub myself up and down a few times, refusing to take my eyes away from Alaska. She's doing something incredibly naughty while she's alone, and I'm getting a front seat for the entire ordeal. I try matching my rhythm to hers as she dips two fingers around the bud between her thighs, tickling and pinching it gently. She squirms and writhes against the tala, moaning as she openly seeks release.

Why is she doing this? It doesn't make sense. Moments ago, she paced frantically and muttered under her breath. And now... she pleasures herself? Why didn't she come to me? I would have happily touched her thighs and nipped her pink, hardened nipples. I would have willingly dragged my tongue along her opening to enjoy all the honey coming out from inside. Why didn't she come to me? *Why? Why? Why?*

Frustration pours through me despite my arousal, and I can no longer keep up with Alaska's slow leisurely pace. I need more. I stroke myself off harder, relieved that Alaska is too focused on her pleasure to realize I'm seeking out my own as well. No longer satisfied stroking myself over my shorts, I sloppily peel them down until they're draped around my ankles. My cock bobs violently, relieved to be set free, and immediately, I circle my length and stroke harder. *Why? Why won't this female speak to me? Why won't she trust me? Why won't she open up to me?* The voice in my head makes me stroke myself to the point of chaffing, but I'm too frustrated to stop.

Alaska shouldn't be making herself come. I should make her come. My mouth should be buried in her folds, not her fingers. Why won't she come to me? Why won't she take our union seriously?

Because it's not a real union.

I grunt, nearly losing it as the voice sends a not-so-gentle reminder of exactly why Alaska won't come to me. It does not matter that we are Chosen mates because it is not real. I said so myself. I told her humans were fragile. I meant it. I told her I didn't want an alien mate. And I meant it. But why do these things not count when it comes to the female fingering herself amongst the talas? Why do I wish to throw away all the rules I've come up with to make her mine? Officially and in all and anyways possible?

None of it should matter. I shouldn't want her. She's human. An alien. A weak, exotic female who has no actual interest in me.

And yet, I can't look away. If she won't let me take my mouth to her… if she would rather make herself cry out instead of letting me, fine. I still need to come. This scene is too erotic for me to stop. I can't look away. Nothing would make me look away now.

Especially when the pressure continues to build. I'm going to come soon. I shouldn't. Not over some female who doesn't care about me. Some weak, frustrating, alien female—

"Oh, Taylis!"

Alaska's cry out shatters my resolve, and I come at the same time as her. It's the hardest I've come in a long time and thick, creamy streams shoot out from my cock and land before me in the grass. Thank the stars Alaska came at the same time because I couldn't stop myself from crying out with release. I keep stroking, replaying the moment I hear Alaska call out my name while she polished herself off. *Me.* She called out for me. She didn't want me there, but she imagined it. It's all so confusing, and impossibly difficult to focus because I'm still shooting my seed across my hands and thighs for a few moments before I'm finally spent and slumped against the tala, breathing hard as though I've just run from a pack of hungry dilewilers.

Once I'm able to catch my breath fully, I use my shorts to clean the seed off my thighs, keeping my eyes on Alaska. She's also slumped to the side and breathing hard. I wonder if she knows what she's done. That she called out for *me.* A flicker of a smile crosses my face because I've never felt more triumphant about being right. She wants me. Of course she does. I was silly to think for even a second that this female isn't seeking me out. The names she's calling out at night don't matter. It doesn't matter that she has night terrors. All that matters is she wants me. *Me.* She called out for me.

"Never took you for a peeping tom."

Startled by the voice, I quickly rise to a standing position, forgetting that my shorts are still beside me on the grass. But Alaska doesn't. After glaring up at me for a few tense moments, she stoops down, retrieves my shorts, and presses them into my waiting hand.

"You might need these," she says coolly. Her hair is disheveled, and her cheeks flushed, but she still manages to hold herself like a graceful high ranked tothid. A society Sidyth. But she can't fool me any longer. Not when I heard her say my name while she came.

Maybe Alaska thinks I didn't hear her. She's undoubtedly holding her chin up high enough to think she's got the upper hand.

"Did you follow me?"

"Yes," I say immediately, taking a step towards her. She takes one back.

"You could have let me know you were following me. It's rude to infringe on a girl's special time."

"You were so loud that I would hardly consider what you were doing *private*." I grin widely, letting every fang show so she realizes I saw and heard everything.

But for some reason, her expression doesn't change. She doesn't look bothered in the least. "I'm a living being just like the next living being. I've got needs."

"You could have come to me for those particular needs." I try reaching for her, but she jumps back at least a hand, maybe two. I allow my hand to fall back to my side casually, refusing to let her win. She thinks I don't know what she said. "Why didn't you come to me when you so obviously wanted me there?"

She scoffs. *Scoffs at me.* "Wanted you there? Why would you say that?"

"I heard you, Alaska," I grumble, tired of verbal sparring. She needs to know that I know.

"You heard me pleasuring myself? Big deal."

"No. *I heard you.* I heard that you said." She cocks her head to the side, further infuriating me, and my scales splay away from my skin in frustration. "What you said. When you came, I heard it. You said my name."

Her expression doesn't change. Doesn't even shift. "You're mistaken, Taylis. Don't flatter yourself."

"I heard you. You said my name when you came. There was no mistake."

"Sorry, Taylis. You're wrong." She spins on her heel, and I'm caught so off guard by her behavior I can't stop myself from stepping forward and circling my hand around her wrist and spinning her back to me.

"You said it," I hiss. "I heard you. Why can't you admit it?"

"There's nothing to admit. Now, let me go."

"Not until you admit you called my name. More importantly, I want to know *why* you did it. Do you want to be Chosen mates?"

"We *are* Chosen mates," she says crisply, and it takes everything I have not to shake her bodily.

"I mean, officially. Do you want me?"

"Does it matter?"

I snarl, and Alaska uses this exact opportunity to wriggle out from my grasp. "Didn't think so. I'm going to head back. Care to join me, or perhaps you'd like to jerk off while I try to have some girl time again?" I expect her to smile. To grin. To do something that reminds me that humans are alien and fragile, but she's just as cool and calm as a Sidyth female, even in heat.

I still taste her arousal in the air. It's incredible.

"You said my name," I snarl, going to follow her.

"Yeah? You can't prove it, can you?"

And that's when it happens.

She breaks out into a smile. I can't tell what kind. It could be cruel. It could be kind. It could be genuine, or it could all just be because this is all a joke to her. But it's there. A smile that reaches up to her eyes, and because of that, I quicken my step to fall in line beside her.

Alaska is the most infuriating, frustrating, alien female I've ever met and will probably ever know.

But it doesn't change the facts. She said my name. I may not be able to prove it, but I'll take it to my death, thinking that she did.

And I liked it.

CHAPTER 6

ALASKA

THAT WAS A CLOSE ONE. I CAN'T BELIEVE I LET MY GUARD DOWN like that for even a single minute. It was foolish. Something the old Alaska would have never allowed to happen. I was careless. I knew Taylis would follow me to the woods. And, yet, while I was trying to work out my frustration, I allowed weakness to take over. I fingered myself in the woods, and the last person who I wanted to be there for it saw the whole thing. Worst of all, he heard me cry out his name.

But it's not for the reason he thinks.

He thinks I'm a silly, horny female, but that's not why I called his name. I called for him because my thoughts had turned dark. I was back on Earth. Back with my stepfather and all his friends. *Like Brady.* The men who cared for me like a daughter. That's the creepiest shit I've ever heard looking back on it. I didn't want any of those old men to be there when I came – not even in my memories. So I called out for Taylis. A familiar face. A friendly face. A face that didn't leer at me while he sought illegal pleasure behind closed doors surrounded by naked Barbie dolls.

Hethdiss is getting to me just like it did to Arizona. I'm growing careless. Comfortable. Convinced my alien pleasure buddy will keep a close eye on me so I have nothing to fear in the woods. Is this how Arizona felt when she realized she had feelings for Drozass? That maybe Hethdiss and the Sidyths aren't as bad as we initially thought? That maybe there could be happiness here? Mates and babies? Security and safety? No more orders, and being in charge of myself for the first time in my entire existence? I'm terrified of it, but not so much so that I would run away from the possibility. I steal a glimpse up at Taylis as he trudges beside me back to the secondary lair.

He's pissed off that I didn't admit I called his name when I came.

Well, boo-fracking-who. I don't have to admit anything. He shouldn't have followed me in the first place, but some small, sick place deep inside knew he would. An even smaller part of me is glad he did. I think it's great he saw me masturbating. That probably pissed him off as well, but he didn't come to stop me. He didn't want me to know that he'd followed me. Which begs the question… is it possible that despite his grumpy behavior, he cares about the fragile human female more than he thought? That his decision to keep me as a Chosen mate is possibly more personal than professional?

I stop right before we enter the open fields facing the secondary and central lair. There's hardly anyone out now, so despite my behavior earlier, I feel I do owe Taylis something.

You could tell him about your past.

I shake Arizona's voice away. *No.* I won't be doing that. Just because I'm becoming more open to the idea of staying on Hethdiss, does not mean I want to give the upper hand to Taylis. He'd probably only use my past against me. Even though I'm a space hussy, I want to believe I'm a space hussy with some dignity, dammit. And sharing a sob story so cliché, it's like something straight out of a *Lifetime* movie isn't exactly on my agenda.

But he deserves something.

"One day, I'll get you to admit it." Taylis' voice rattles me back to the present, and I stare at him. "You said my name. If you admit it now, I won't even be upset that you pleasured yourself when you could have easily come to me."

"Does it bother you that much that I didn't? A girl likes to take care of herself sometimes, you know."

"I don't like it," he says, forcing my eyes to widen. "When you want pleasure, you should come to your mate. *I* will happily make you come."

I arch an eyebrow, not bothering to hide my skepticism. He can't possibly be serious. "Every time I ask?"

"Every time." There's no hesitation in his voice.

It's hard not to smile at him. Jesus, that's two smiles in one day. I'm losing my touch. For years, all I've ever known is accepting orders to avoid drama. It was notably worse because even if I did fight orders, something worse would happen and I would end up having to follow the orders anyway. Hearing that it's okay for me to order someone around makes me warm up to Taylis even more, even though I know it's such a bad idea to let my guard down completely with him.

"Is that what being a Chosen mate is all about?" I ask carefully. "Making the other one come whenever they ask? Sounds like a lot of coming if you ask me." I dare to look up at Taylis, but his face has returned to that stoic and grumpy expression. But it doesn't make him any less attractive. He may look grouchy, but he's never looked cruel. He doesn't have the same look in his eyes like so many other clients of my past. "We could have done this as pleasure mates, right?"

"We could have."

"But you wanted to become Chosen mates to keep me safe."

"Correct. But—"

"But?" My heart leaps for some reason, and I interrupt him before he has the chance to finish. When he doesn't start to speak again, I lower my head. "But we're only Chosen mates in name to keep me safe. That's what you were going to say."

"That's not what I was going to say."

"So tell me." I dare to reach out and brush my fingertips against his wrist. He just watched me masturbate, but this touch feels so much more intimate. And not only for me. He shivers against my fingers, and a few scales splay away from his thick forearms. "Please, Taylis. I didn't mean to interrupt. Just… say what you were going to say. We're Chosen mates to keep me safe, but?"

My words hang in the air, and the silence makes me break out into a cold sweat. I swear I hear strange rustling in the woods around us, but I can't think about that now. I have a mate. I'm not like Arizona. Even if some other Sidyth was around, watching us, he wouldn't dare take me. Taylis said so himself. I'm safe now. I'm mated.

So why does it feel like someone's watching us?

Before I have a chance to think on this too deeply, Taylis pulls his arm away from my hand and seizes my wrist. He yanks me to his chest, and I buckle from the impact, surprised he would be so rough. But when my eyes meet his, I see there's nothing dangerous in his expression.

"You are a very frustrating alien," he says, frowning.

"So are you," I remind him sharply. "You're an alien—"

"Human females are supposed to be fragile and emotional. They are weak—"

"We're not weak."

"But not you," he interrupts. "You are none of these things. You're emotionless. You're calm, and you're cool. You rarely show joy or anger: frustration or sadness. I don't know what to make of it. When you are awake, you are impossible to read."

"When I'm awake?" I ask, catching his strange wording.

"At night, you are more vulnerable." Without warning, he wraps both arms around my waist and our chests touch. Heat rises to my face and parts of my body a little further south, but I try not to focus on that. "You cry out at night. You say names that do not translate. You thrash about, Alaska. I want to know why."

I try lowering my eyes. "I don't know what you're talking about."

He pulls my chin upward, forcing our eyes to meet once again. It's such a soft and gentle touch that it makes my eyes water for some reason. He notices my distress and loosens his grip, but not enough for me to escape. *Of course not.* His eyes seared into mine, begging, pleading for an answer. He wants to know about my past. Arizona thinks I should tell him. Ugh, but I don't think I can do it. Taylis is worried he can't take a human female as a mate because they're weak and fragile. I've only held his attention this long because of my stoic demeanor.

Hearing about Tanner could change all of that in a heartbeat.

"You must feel comfortable with me, Alaska." His grip is now loose enough for me to escape, but I can't bring myself to move away. Not when he's so focused on me. Completely. His words are gruff, but not careless. His expression is hard but not cruel. He says I should treat him as though we are Chosen mates, yet constantly reminds me that we are doing this only for my protection. Taylis is a walking, talking contradiction, and it's driving me crazy. "You need to open up to me, Alaska. If you do not, I will stop at nothing to figure out what is bothering you."

"Is that a threat?" I straighten my spine, using all 5'10" of my frame against his, but it's useless considering he's an inch or two shy of seven feet. I don't mind being ordered around, but I don't like being threatened.

"It's a promise," he says in a low voice. "I want you to open up to me in all ways."

"Because we're Chosen mates?"

"Exactly."

"That's too damn bad," I hiss, finally finding the courage to pull my body away from his. "We're mates in name only, in case you forgot." More trees rustle behind Taylis, but I'm convinced it's just the wind. "I'm going back to the lair. See you later." I start to turn, but his voice breaks through my resolve like a pick shattering ice.

"No. Stay here."

I freeze in my spot, hating that I don't want to fight against him. It's like I can't resist an order. His voice is so low, so deep. So commanding. It reminds me of my stepfather's but without the disregard for my body. Taylis would never hurt me. Maybe that's why I listen to him. I'm not afraid of what will happen if I run. Perhaps he'll chase me, but he won't pin me down to the bed, tie my arms and legs to the posts with an argyle tie and use a worn business sock to suppress my screams. I'm not used to hearing a voice making demands while still respecting me.

I want more.

"Why?" I dare to ask, keeping my back to him. "Are you going to ask me to make you come now? Since I won't ask you?"

"You know I wouldn't do that to you."

I hear him take a step closer. The hairs on the back of my neck stand at attention, feeling his looming presence. "You could, you know. I'm yours in every way. Client. Pleasure mate. Chosen mate. You can have me however you want. Whenever you want."

"Does that mean I can ask anything of you?" He takes another step, and careful fingers brush my hip bone. A small moan escapes my lips as the hand circles around me possessively, and Taylis pulls my back against his chest. His chin is so high he can't even rest it on the top of my head.

"Anything, sexual, yes."

"And if I want more? If I want to know about why you scream in the night?"

"I can't tell you that."

"You're my mate, Alaska."

"In name only."

He hisses loudly, and his hands release from my skin. "You are so incredibly frustrating."

"So are you," I hiss back, darting around him and heading in the opposite direction of the lairs. It feels good to run, to feel a piece of freedom. Low hanging branches scratch me on the cheeks, but I don't give a damn. I need to do something for myself. And not to be an asshole, but I know Taylis wouldn't dare leave me alone. Even now, his feet are pounding behind me along with another set.

I stop in my tracks. *Another set?*

The crashing ahead of me quiets, and Taylis lifts me off the ground from behind and turns back towards the lairs. It all happens so quickly that I almost miss the shadows hanging back. They're standing in the direction I was heading, and if I had kept running, I would have most likely met the owners of the shadows.

Other Sidyths.

My heart hiccups with Taylis' bounding gait, but I'm too shaken to fight him. For the first time, I feel genuinely safe in his arms. Taylis jogs back to the secondary lair with me draped over his shoulder like a sack of potatoes, and I'm in too much of a daze to say anything. My mind is reeling at the memory of those shadows in the woods. They reminded me too much of when my bedroom door would open after my stepfather tied me down. His friends would stop by late, and though my room would be dark, the hall outside would be brightly lit, so they would only look like shadows at first.

When Taylis' steps finally come to a halt, we're back in his lair, and he sets me down on the bed roughly. I watch as he pulls the curtain shut and keeps his back to me. His shoulders are tightly bunched, his hands in fists. He hasn't said anything yet either, and his silence worries me.

Did he see what I saw? Did he know others were watching us? Did he know how close I was to being caught by them?

Taylis turns, and though I shouldn't be surprised, I'm also taken aback by how angry his expression is. He's fuming when our eyes meet.

"I knew humans were fragile, but I did not know they were stupid," he hisses, making me slide back further on his bed. I expect him to punish me somehow, but he keeps his distance. "You do not run into the talas. You do not leave the comfort of the lair boundaries. What part of high alert escaped your memory in that moment of stupidity?"

"I don't know," I mutter, wishing I could go back in time. I want to run again towards the lairs so Taylis won't look at me the way he's looking at me now.

"You don't want to speak about your past? Fine. But I did not think you had a death wish."

"Death wish?" I croak.

"Did you not feel it?" he hisses. "There were others. Watching. Observing. Those males are not my brothers. Not Prince Korben's either. Not anymore. And you ran to them. Ran! Like you were so desperate that you would rather become a sexual plaything to strangers than speak to me about your night terrors! How does this make sense?"

"It doesn't," I grumble, feeling the weight of my mistake truly. Taylis isn't only angry. He's worried. About me. It only makes me feel worse. I shouldn't have run from him. I should have run back towards the lairs.

"Scheita," he grumbles, pushing a hand through his short, dark hair.

"So, there were others?" I dare to ask him.

"Of course there were others! Did you not feel their desperation?"

"We're mated—"

"Those males do not care," he says quickly, and then immediately clamps his mouth shut and composes himself with a grave sigh. "You do not understand. You alien females think you are invincible when you are actually, weak, fragile, and stupid."

"I made a mistake, Taylis. I didn't know."

"You didn't know you were running from me instead of speaking to me?" His eyes lift, still furious.

"Well." I shrink back. "I did know that."

"You would rather belong to someone else then."

"That's *not* what I'm saying." I rise from the bed but keep my distance. "I made a mistake, Taylis. I'm sorry. I didn't think… you said we were safe."

"I know I did. But it's still complicated."

"Tell me why."

"Tell me why you would rather run then speak to me." His shoulders slack as he faces me fully. "Why do you run rather than talk? Is it as Chentan says? Are you masking another emotion with anger?"

"Chentan? Did you speak to him about me? About us?"

"What else could I do? Alaska, you may not realize this, but you have been thrashing about in the bed for many passings and saying strange names. Fighting and screaming. Crying. When I ask you about it, you say you will not speak to me. You grow angry. I wanted to help you."

"Why?" I hiss.

"You are my Chosen mate."

"In name only."

"Fine! Then it is also because I care about you."

"Care about me? But—"

"As a female in my care," he says clumsily.

My expression darkens. "A whore."

"An *alien female*," he returns. "In my care. I don't want you to feel unsafe when you are with me. I will die protecting you, Alaska. You must understand this, yes?" When I try lowering my head, Taylis finally feels calm enough to advance on me again, resting heavy hands on each of my shoulders. Once again, my eyes water for reasons I cannot understand, but Taylis holds my gaze, as intense as ever. "You may not be so different than the others," he says in a low voice.

"What... what does that mean?"

"This." Slowly he reaches up, and for a split second, I'm afraid he's going to slap me for not listening to an order. This is why I should listen. I should always listen to orders when they're given because this is what always happens in the end when I don't. I pinch my eyes shut, preparing myself for a strike, but there's only a whisper of touch across my cheekbone. I slowly open my eyes, and to my shock, there's a drop of moisture on the pad of Taylis' pointer finger. I swallow hard, but he only flicks it away. "I don't like seeing you like this. I know I am the cause, but you must understand... I don't... I don't know what I want. Not anymore."

"What... what do you mean?" I ask, trying not to sound as perplexed as I feel. My throat feels dry and tight.

"You are a human female, and you are different, but not that much so. And though I never wanted an alien for a mate, you are so much more than an alien." He shakes his head, obviously frustrated. "When you ran from me, something tore in my chest. I felt shattered. Broken. Destroyed. Does that sound like someone who wants you as a mate in name only?" Despite his confused expression, I can't help but smile cautiously.

He cares. Fuck me; he cares about me. Maybe more so than he thought.

I shouldn't allow it, but I feel myself growing giddy despite maintaining a cautious expression.

"I think…" I trail off, trying to find the right words, but this whole situation has left me so drained that I take a seat back on the bed. "I think I need to lay down."

His expression drops slightly. "I will join you then."

"It's your bed. You can do whatever you want."

"It's *our* bed."

As I lay down, he quietly follows, and there are so many things I wish I could speak to him about.

I want to ask him about the other Sidyths in the woods. Why they're different than the ones Chocal tried to sell Arizona to. He said they're different. That they don't care if I'm mated. It's a lot to take in. And though I should mostly focus on that, a small part of me would rather kiss Taylis and demand him to tell me what he meant when he said I'm more than an alien female.

Does he want to be more than Chosen mates by name?

What would that mean for me? What would that mean for him? Why's he so against it in the first place?

And why the fuck do I care so much?

I thought that after my conversation with Arizona that things would become more apparent. But I'm more confused than ever. Taylis confuses me. My past confuses me.

But a possible future with Taylis? That confuses me most of all.

CHAPTER 7

TAYLIS

ALASKA DOESN'T HAVE NIGHT TERRORS AFTER SHE NEARLY RAN straight into the arms of some *outsiders*. Which may be a good thing, because I cannot sleep. My mind is too restless. Not only with the prospect of losing her but *caring* so much about the possibility of losing her. When she ran from me, my entire world shifted into slow motion. Each step took her further away from me — right to where those *arslotas* waited — probably salivating at the idea of taking away a human. I knew this would happen eventually. Prince Korben played a shaky hand when he brought in so many alien females at once, and now things are starting to change.

The calm *outsiders* are growing more curious.

The more rebellious, wild outsiders are growing more aggressive in their pursuits.

I stare down at Alaska as she sleeps peacefully beside me in bed. The sun rayers beam down on her tan, golden scaleless skin, but it doesn't detract from her beauty. Her beauty was never alien to me. Despite her strange, small features, clawless fingers, I always found her beautiful. Her skin is not blue, but I like her golden skin. I love her full breasts and her skeptical sneers. She's one of the taller females here, but she's not slim and muscular like a Sidyth female. She has curves that look perfectly placed on her round, soft frame, and her slinky black top clings to her breasts as though trying to escape. I nearly groan with need, but I'm also relieved to see Alaska sleeping soundlessly right now.

There are no signs of terrors. Whatever horrors await in her subconsciousness, have decided to leave her alone for the time being.

I am glad for that, but it doesn't set my mind enough at ease to fall asleep beside her.

There are too many unanswered questions. I am almost speaking more strangely than she has been behaving. What is wrong with me? Am I serious about wanting to take an alien for a mate? Giving up everything waiting for me back on the fatherland? My life on Sidetha wasn't perfect, but it was a decent. Comfortable. And this term of exile was only supposed to be temporary. But now, here I am, considering a future and forever with an icy, human female who won't even share how she feels about me or the memories that haunt her while she sleeps.

I don't know how much time has passed when Alaska groans softly, and her eyes flutter open. When she notices me staring down at her, I am pleasantly surprised by the hint of arousal that wafts up from between her thighs and straight into my nostrils. I smile down at her.

"Jesus," she mutters. "How long have I been asleep?"

"No idea."

"What time is it?"

"Don't know. If you're still tired, you're more than welcome to sleep." I notice her eyes grow hooded for some reason, and it takes everything I have not to ask her if she'd like me to pleasure her.

She shakes her head. "N-no. I'm all right. Just surprised."

"That you didn't have night terrors?" I ask her carefully.

"Yeah." Her answer is simple, giving me no room to ask further questions. "No nightmares. Have you been awake this whole time?"

"I think so."

"Huh. What have you been doing? Just creepily watching me sleep?"

"I don't find it creepy to observe my mate while she's resting." I shrug.

She arches an eyebrow. "You didn't do anything to me, did you? Sexually?"

Horror strikes me. "What? No! You were resting peacefully. I would never." I rarely raise my voice, but something about her question bothers me. She asked her question so seriously. Which makes me wonder... "Has something like that happened to you before?"

Her eyes widen, and she glances away. I lower my chin, and I swear there's a hint of color flashing across her usually colorless cheeks. It catches me off guard.

"Does that make you angry?"

"Of course it does."

"With me? If someone did something like to me in the past would you be upset with me—"

I hiss loudly. "I would be *upset* with whatever arslota would try anything sexual with a defenseless, fragile human female." I can't help leaning closer to her on the bed, and though her eyes dart wildly back and forth, she doesn't move away, and white heat rises up my spine. "Did this happen to you, Alaska? Did one of your past clients..."

She shakes her head. "Even if they did, it wouldn't have bothered me. They paid for it."

"But it's happened." Her eyes grow glassy. Despite my anger, the vision of her emotions sends a bolt of excitement right to my cock. She isn't so cold after all. She isn't an android. She's a female. A human female. And someone touched her inappropriately. "You don't have to tell me if you don't want to. All right? I'm not going to force you." Relief washes across her features, and though I should be happy to see it, curiosity still bites at me.

She said it happened with clients, but that it didn't matter.

Which means… it happened on her homeworld.

Someone… one of her kin… touched her while she rested?

No wonder she had night terrors.

Without speaking a word, I reach out and pull Alaska right against my body. A muffled cry escapes her lips, but she doesn't fight. She curls up closer, nuzzling her face against my chest. My cock tingles and bobs in my shorts, begging to be set free to pound inside Alaska's cunt, but now is not the time. Alaska has not said much about her past, but this behavior means so much more than words. My female is… damaged. Someone has hurt her. Made her feel unsafe to sleep. *Someone touched her inappropriately.*

"Sorry." Her warm breath brushes against my skin, and I maneuver my hips so I'm not stabbing her in the stomach with my erect cock.

"You have nothing to be sorry about," I mutter into her hair, wishing I could offer more. But I need to know. It's like a drug. If she would only tell me about her past, I would do everything I could to fix it. I could help her feel better. "If you want to talk, I will listen. If you wish to remain silent, I will listen to the sound of your hearts beating and your soft breathing."

"Humans only have one heart," she says.

"How odd." I curl up my nose in disgust, trying to push this strange thought away from my mind while my human leans on me. She may never do it again. That's what makes the moment so special and yet so terrifying. "The choice is yours, Alaska. You can tell me what you want. Anything you want. Or nothing at all. But the choice is yours."

"The choice is mine." My words sound alien coming from her small, pink lips, but I am happy, at least, to feel that she is considering them. "Do you have a family back home, Taylis?"

"This is what you wish to speak about?"

"Please."

I take in a deep sigh and release it slowly. "Yes. I have family back on the fatherland."

"Are they happy? Are you happy? Do they love you?"

"They are not unhappy, and neither am I," I say. "And love is a strange thing on the fatherland. I would be more likely to say I am respected."

She hums thoughtfully. "And your parents? Do they respect you?"

"Yes. That is why I am here. To earn their respect." I frown, expecting her to pry, but wherever this conversation is headed, is not what I'm assuming, I'm sure.

"Your mom and your dad? You have both?"

"They're both alive."

"I see. My mom died at a young age. I don't know who my dad is."

"You don't *know*?" I can't help the judgment in my voice. "How can you not know? He is your life giver! Without him, there would be no you."

An uncomfortable laugh erupts from her chest, but I don't think there's anything funny. More importantly, I'm confused about what any of this has to do with her night terrors or her kin touching her inappropriately while she sleeps. The impatient part of me wants to ask her straight out where she's going with this, but at the same time, I don't want the moment to end. She's in my arms. Pressing up against me and despite her words, she's enjoying being close. I can tell by her scent. This is the most open Alaska has ever been with me, and so, despite wanting to know how this story will begin or end, I relax and try focusing on her words, her scent, and not her erotic taste on my tongue.

"Yeah, it's kind of weird, I guess. No dad. I did have my mom for a little while. Until I was… I think nine? Maybe ten. It's hard to remember."

"You were alone at such a young age?"

Another uncomfortable laugh. "No. Not exactly. Though honestly, maybe that would have been better." She clears her throat. "No, my mom remarried right before she died. I had a stepfather."

"Step… father?"

"It's like a second father. My original one wasn't around, but Mom wanted me to have a father figure in my life, I guess. She married… Tanner." She says the name with a bit of disgust, and it's a sound I recognize almost immediately. I've heard her say this name before.

Along with others. In her night terrors. "He was almost ten years younger than my mom, so really, he wasn't that much older than I am now." She shrugs, burying her face more deeply into my chest as though she doesn't want me to see her expression.

I'm aching for her to go on, but I'm also enjoying her touch. I wrap an arm tightly around her back as to somehow keep us even closer, and I'm shocked when she doesn't struggle. This isn't the Alaska I've known for over a year. I've never held her this long. She's never allowed me to. And yet now, in this instant, she's pressed up against me like she never wants me to let her go.

"Tanner… freaked me out from the start," Alaska starts again. "He was big. He worked in construction, and he had a bunch of friends who were big like him." I feel her twitch. "Not as big as you guys, but as a child, they looked ten feet tall to me. They would lift and swing me around, and most of them didn't care if I liked or hated it. If they wanted to touch me, they would. And it was mostly innocent, so my mother never stopped them. Until she died."

I swallow deeply, noticing for the first time that despite Alaska's strong, calm demeanor, that she's so soft and fragile under my hands. I try to picture her so much younger and smaller than she is now and some of my rougher, more callous brothers messing around with her. Alaska screaming to be put down, but her words ignored. After a while, she probably just dealt with it because it used less energy than yelling. "What happened then?"

"After she died... *fuck*... Tanner's friends started coming over more and more. Some of them liked me. A lot. I guess I liked the attention at first, but sometimes it got to be overwhelming. I missed Mom." She sniffs, and I nearly lose my breath. "I tried telling one of the nicer guys that... Brady... and he said there was a way he could help me forget." She lifts her head. "You have to understand; I was only ten, Taylis. Only ten. I didn't know he would—"

"Continue," I say gruffly, needing to hear the end of her tale like a male needs a drink after a long hot trip in a desert. "What did he do? How did he help you feel better?" *Brady.* Another familiar name. One Alaska has screamed out before. The thrashing. The tears. The begging for it all to stop. I swallow a hard lump in my throat. "You were only two hands old?"

"Y-yes," she says, shaking.

"How old was he?"

She jolts. "At least four... h-hands, that is. Maybe five hands." She holds up her hands and I count the fingers in my head. Five hands worth of fingers. "I can't remember."

"A full-grown male... and a sprog."

"He was nicer than some of the other guys who hung out with

my stepfather. He always looked at me, and I guess I thought it was because he cared so much. When he said he could help me forget about Mommy—err, my mom, I jumped at the chance. He told me to wait in the basement for him. A small room in the corner. It locked from the inside and the outside. He said to wait there while Tanner and the rest of his friends went to a bar. Then we would be alone for a few minutes, and Tanner wouldn't have to know."

I feel myself gripping Alaska more tightly, maybe even painfully so, but I can't help myself. I can barely understand where this is going, but something about this story doesn't feel right. Doesn't seem possible. Full-grown males do not touch sprogs sexually. It is just… wrong. My mind twists painfully trying to understand the possibility. But there can be no other way for this story to end. Not with the way Alaska has set it up.

The questions Alaska asked about kin and family.

The fear of being touched inappropriately.

The fear of not following orders.

Giving up on fighting because it was simply easier to let bad things happen.

"I went down to the basement and waited for him," Alaska continues. "God, I was so excited. Brady was going to help me feel better. That's all I wanted. I heard him upstairs talking to Tanner and his friends, and I don't even think Tanner asked about me. Maybe he knew what Brady wanted. Maybe he didn't care. Either way, I remember the door shutting and all but dancing around in excitement for when Brady would come downstairs." Another deep sigh. "I was so stupid."

"You were young," I whisper, kissing her hair. "What you are telling me? Please tell me it is not what I am thinking."

"What are you thinking?"

"Did he touch you?" I can't help snarling at the question. "This full-grown male? Did he touch you?"

She doesn't answer. She doesn't have to. Her reaction is clear. And though I'm still having a difficult time processing, it seems my worst fears were correct. A full-grown male touched her. Inappropriately. And her second father… this Tanner… might have known about it. Such a concept is so foreign and horrific I almost lose my breath.

And now, I know.

Alaska isn't some weak, fragile human female. She's strong. So strong for not letting something like this ruin her. She works and walks every day with her head held high. Thinking… maybe even assuming other males will touch her. As an Intergalactic Call-Girl, she's had no reason to change her reasoning. Males have touched her inappropriately. And she's always assumed it's better to not fight with a nasty result than to fight and receive an ugly punishment, and then an even more unpleasant result. And she takes it. She lives with this thought every moment of every day. And for whatever reason, lately, she hasn't been able to suppress these memories. They've come to the surface.

What scares me most of all is, I don't think this is the last time one of her second father's friends touched her. "You don't have to say another word," I say firmly. Not only for her sake but mine. I'm so angry I'm afraid what I'll do if I see one of my brothers. I'll spar anyone right now. I'll fight Hujun and Azan at the same time with the way I'm feeling right now. Just to let off some of my frustration.

"Thank you." Her words barely reach my ears, but I hear relief in her tone. She snuggles more deeply as though I'm the one keeping her sane. Maybe I am. Maybe telling me part of her story is what's doing it. I suppose it doesn't matter. She's here with me now, and she's safe. Now and forever. I'll never let another male touch her.

Not one of my brothers.

Not one of the *outsiders*.

Not another alien.

And indeed, not the arslota kin who touched her at such a young age.

No. I want her with me now. Always. As a pleasure mate. A Chosen mate.

I can't have her as a Chosen mate in name only anymore. It's not enough. I need to have all of her. I need to take in her all her horrors so I can share a small piece of her pain. I want to shoulder some of her fears and burdens. Be sad with her. Be angry with her. There's no one else I could imagine being with now. I can't return home to the fatherland if it means someone else will get their claws or tentacles on this fragile, yet simultaneously strong human female. I don't care about the fatherland — my father or mother's approval. I don't need any of it because without knowing Alaska is safe, none of it matters.

Now, I need her to understand that. Understand my feelings for her have changed.

But not tonight. Not now. Right now, I want her to feel safe in my arms. Ready and able to share anything else she wants. I won't burden her with talk of becoming true Chosen mates. In my mind, she already belongs to me. Maybe she's always belonged to me, even if I wasn't ready to acknowledge it.

All I know is that I'm desperate now to show her that males can be good. We can be kind and gentle and patient. And though our words may be gruff, it doesn't mean our actions will be. I want to give her a family filled with the kindness she had only for a limited amount of time while her mother was still alive. I never gave much thought to sprogs before, but now I'll be happy to provide Alaska with as many as she wants to build a family she can love deeply and will love her deeply in return.

I'll give all of that to her, but she still must let me. She's taken a considerable step tonight by trusting me with just a fraction of her horrific past. But to love her truly, she must learn to love me.

Not as a protector or as a client. But as a lover. Someone who will worship and treat her better than any other male in her past.

One day she will be mine in every way a female can belong to her mate and vice versa.

But not tonight.

Tonight, I want Alaska to relax. Feel the safety I can provide.

Consider a future even I never considered until this moment.

An alien for a Chosen mate. Really and truly.

CHAPTER 8

ALASKA

I HAVEN'T HAD NIGHTMARES FOR SEVERAL NIGHTS NOW. IT'S odd because I'm still not entirely at ease. It's been so long since I've spoken about my past, but it still rings so fresh in my mind. Like Tanner is right beyond Taylis' lair opening – waiting to take me back home to the little room in the basement, or my bedroom with the pink sheets and rainbow comforter. Things are getting better. I can't pretend they're not, but I can't help but notice the fewer night terrors I have, the more uneasy I grow during the day.

Taylis has been surprisingly patient about the whole ordeal. I leave out most of the gory details not only because I don't want him to hear them, but because I don't want to listen to them. Hearing them out loud makes them too real. Too painful. Too likely to happen once again. But I appreciate Taylis' change. He's more patient lately. He doesn't rush me, and when I want to speak to Arizona, he doesn't mind.

I wonder if I should tell Arizona what's happening. Not only about Taylis and myself, but the *outsiders* who don't care if a human female is mated or not. There's still plenty of women on Hethdiss who don't have a mate following them around, and I know for a fact that the workout twins like jogging around the borders every morning, noon, and night. But for some reason, it's not on my mind as much as it should be. Because all I can think about is Taylis and how he's accepting every part of me. And he seems more open to choosing an *alien* as an official mate, and not just to keep me safe.

Which he's pretty much doing around the clock anyway.

For the first time since Mom died, and then again when I met Arizona for the first time, I feel safe and like someone truly has my back and is going to protect me. I think Taylis wants to be someone special in my life, and I'm surprised by how much I'm all for that, as well.

Deciding that I've hidden in his lair long enough, I tell Taylis I'm going outside for some fresh air. He arches a skeptical eyebrow but lets me go. I think he knows I don't mind being ordered around, so long as I feel like I'm not leashed and collared by his side. But I can tell he's worried about me being out of his sight. I promise I'm only going to the secondary Gathering Room, even if it is only to sit and listen to other conversations, and he seems satisfied enough with this that he lets me go.

I'm walking past some of the private lairs though when I notice a familiar voice. Arizona's mate. Drozass. He's talking to someone else. I think Kansas and Dakota's mates – who are idiots, if you ask me, and their voices carry into the hallways, making it almost impossible not to want to stop and listen. All right, they're not talking that quietly, but it's rare to see so many males around here without their mates. Dragging my steps as much as I can, I try catching bits and pieces of their conversation.

"Another delivery is coming soon. We need to prepare ourselves for an attack." It's Dakota's mate – Cade. Sounding as cocky as ever. "You heard what Taylis said. And you too, for that matter, Drozass. They know there are females here. They want their own. And the only way to get them is to bargain with the male who delivers the next stock." My ears perk up at this at the same time my stomach drops. Taylis spoke to them? About what? And how much? I stop entirely just beyond the curtain to hear more. "Drozass, your foolish female ran off once—"

"She did not runoff. Chocal tricked her."

"Either way," Cade continues. "It's only a matter of time before another female is *tricked* again. Taylis already worries about it. The rest of us should be worried, as well. That dead-eyed female nearly ran off into the arms of a bunch of *outsiders*! So stupid. It could happen again, and I'm not about to lose my female because Taylis' mate is so desperate to get away from him—"

"Stop," Drozass hisses. "We don't know what happened. Don't tell wild stories, Cade."

"All I'm saying is we need to prepare. You know *outsiders* are going to be watching and waiting for the next delivery. They'll want to see if they can have some of their own females brought in. I'm sure they've been working hard to build something of value."

"We will speak with Prince Korben on the matter," Drozass says firmly.

"He won't do anything," another hisses. Kansas' mate. Dash. "The time of words is over. It is time for action to protect these females!"

"I will speak to Taylis again," Drozass says. "He says things are getting better with his female. I have no reason to believe she will foolishly run off again." My heart pounds heavily against my top. Taylis told them what happened. He told them! I feel so embarrassed and ashamed. And *betrayed.* "We will figure things out and make the appropriate decisions. I agree that things need to change. More males grow curious. More careless about the rules of the fatherland. We will speak with Prince Korben and tell him what happened with Taylis' mate and—"

I storm away, not wanting to hear another word. I don't even know why I'm so upset. Of course, Taylis spoke to his brothers. Of course, he wants to help keep everyone safe. But the way his brothers spoke about me, based on what Taylis said? He makes me sound like an idiot. A fool. A foolish human female. *Which is probably still how he sees me.*

Frowning, I return to Taylis' lair, hoping he isn't there. But he straightens up in bed when I return, rising to his feet.

"Don't get up." I maneuver around him so I can lay back down in bed without another word to him.

"Are you all right?"

"Fine. Just realized I didn't need fresh air, after all. I need to sleep some more."

"I see." There's shifting behind me, and though I'm dying to figure out what he's doing, I pinch my eyes shut, still thinking about how Cade and Dash spoke about me. How Taylis must have talked about me to his brothers. When there are rustling and a few light footsteps, I realize Taylis must be leaving his lair. "I have to take care of something. Would you like me to stay with you?"

"No."

Another few footsteps. I feel his presence looming over mine in bed. "Is something bothering you?"

"Yes," I grumble. "I'm tired, and I'm trying to sleep, and you're talking my ear off. Do you mind?"

He doesn't say another word, but footsteps exit the lair. I'm alone. He's probably going to speak with his brothers — more about his foolish female. I don't know why I'm surprised. Sidyths are aliens. They're alien clients. Prince Korben – for all his *noble* intentions, bought Intergalactic Call-Girls to mate with his brothers. He purchased them wives. His brothers should have no reason to respect us. We're hired and paid for. They can talk about us how they like. Use us how they want. Just like things are supposed to be. Like they used to be.

I thought I found someone who could take the lead now that Arizona no longer feels worthy. I was foolish to believe it could be Taylis. He can't lead me. He doesn't even respect me.

I flip over in bed, snarling under my breath because I'm not sure what to do with myself. Now that Taylis is gone, I'm antsy. Hell, maybe I should have gone outside for some fresh air, after all. Perhaps I should take my chances with other Sidyth males. It can't hurt any worse than it hurts right now. I'm used to being abused. I'm not used to being cherished. And Taylis made me feel just that. And it hurts because it must have all been a lie.

So stupid, Cade had said when speaking about me. He even took it back when Drozass mentioned that Chocal tricked Arizona, and not merely running away. But that wasn't the case for me. I ran because I wanted to get away. Just like Cade said. Just like Taylis must have told him. It makes me wonder if Taylis is the only one who feels about humans like he does. Does that fool, Cade, think humans are primitive and flighty? Does Drozass? The idea of Arizona giving up everything to be with a male who doesn't respect humans makes me angry.

Can the *outsiders* beyond our borders any different?

Would I feel more at home in an environment with an owner who barked orders at me with no thoughts of me disobeying? Would I feel more comfortable with that?

Yes. Well, maybe to start. But after only a year spent on Hethdiss with exiled Sidyths, I can't help but wonder if I've changed. I realize it's been a pretty long time not taking orders from anyone. Arizona herself mentioned that I've changed.

Maybe she's right. I want to make decisions on my own… I think. But it's never ended up good.

I pull the covers over my head as a painful memory awakens within my mind.

"WHAT IS GOING ON HERE?" THE VOICE SHOUTING AT ME FROM across the room sounds angry, and yet somewhat familiar. Brady is hunched over me, and removes his hand from under my blouse, turning lazily in the direction of the voice.

It's Tanner. He's in the doorframe, his face is red and flushed. His massive fists are curled tightly into balls, and he's glaring at the scene before him. Brady has me on the floor.

"Daddy," I whisper, regardless of how Tanner always said I should call him by his first name. "Daddy, he—"

"I told you to lock the door," he hisses, entering the room and shutting the door behind him. "Anyone could come in here."

"I'm sorry, Tanner," Brady huffs. "Just got so excited."

"Unbelievable." His light brown eyes won't meet mine as he takes a seat in the corner of the room. He's got a glass in his hand, filled with amber liquid and ice cubes. He doesn't say anything to me but takes a calm, leisurely drink.

I'm stunned when Brady turns away from Tanner and snakes his hand up my blouse again.

"Please," I beg, for the first time wanting this to stop. Brady's touches usually didn't bother me, but something about Tanner watching made me feel flushed and embarrassed. "I don't… I don't think I like this anymore."

"Shut up." Brady pinches me roughly, making me cry out, eyes watering. "We can do this the hard way or the easy way. I suggest you choose easy."

I writhe under his calloused hands, and my stepfather remains silent. But curiosity plagues me anyway. "What's the hard way?"

Brady chuckles. "Fight me; I'll punish you. And I'll still get what I want. If you don't fight me, I won't punish you."

"But you'll still get what you want."

Brady whistles. "She's a smart one, isn't she, Tanner?"

He doesn't respond to his friend.

I don't bother fighting. Not if the outcome will be the same, no matter what.

"Amy," Brady growls, dipping his hand lower to the place that makes me uncomfortable. "You are a beautiful girl. And good little girls do as men ask. You don't want to be a naughty girl, do you?" I shake my head, hating the idea of it. "Your daddy thinks you're a perfect girl, letting me do this. And I need this, Amy. Need you."

I want to smile. Despite the discomfort from Brady's invasive fingers, I want to smile because he's right in a way. I want Tanner to like me. I want him to be like the daddies at school. Maybe if I do what Brady wants, he'll be happy. He'll be pleased with me. Then I can ask him to make Brady stop one day.

"Shut up," Tanner grumbles. "I don't want her calling me daddy." The vision shatters as my stepfather stands suddenly and goes to exit the room. "I'm locking the door, Brady. Be a little smarter next time, all right?"

"Yes, sir," Brady grunts, returning to his work.

STARTLED, I RISE IN BED, FEELING COLD SWEAT DRIP DOWN MY temple despite the hot temperature and humidity in the lair. I must have fallen asleep. My mind relaxed. And because of that, now I'm thinking about Brady. Tanner. My stepfather. The man who let others touch me because he... I don't want to think about it and scrub a hand down my face. God, there's so much Taylis doesn't know about me. He knows some, but I bet he'd never call me a foolish human if he had to go through half the shit I went through.

I glance down at the sheets and shove them away, hating that they smell like sex. It's nauseating now. I need to get away, and quickly rise to my feet and shuffle towards the opening until I collide right with a broad, blue chest.

"Alaska." It's Taylis. His golden eyes are wide with shock. "What is—"

"Amy," I mutter, shaking my head.

"Huh?"

"My name isn't Alaska, you know. It's Amy."

He seems more perplexed than ever, going to reach for my shoulders, but I stumble back into the lair, collapsing on the end of his bed.

"What is wrong? Please. You are speaking nonsense. You are sweating. Did you have another night terror?"

"No." The lie instantly flows from my lips, and I'm not about to take it back.

"Lies." Without asking permission, Taylis advances on me with a hungry look in his eyes. Almost predatorial. I back away until I smack into the headboard, and Taylis holds up a hand. "I'm not going to hurt you. What is wrong? Seriously? Amy?"

My eyes dart upward at the sound of my old name. And I realize... almost instantaneously, that I don't want that name any longer. It's too painful. Just hearing it uttered by Taylis makes me shiver. "D-don't," I say in a trembling voice. "I... I made a mistake."

"You said that was your name?" He still seems confused. His eyes seared into mine. "Amy—"

"NO!" I bellow. "I don't want to be called that! I'm Alaska! Alaska!"

"All right," he rumbles over me. "Alaska."

"I'm Alaska... not Amy." I pull my knees up to my chest, and rock slowly, trying to push the memories of Tanner and Brady out of my mind. But they're here now. Leering. Laughing. The rattle of ice cubes rings as freshly in my ears as church bells on a Sunday. "Not Amy," I say, looking up at Taylis as he moves closer. "Not Amy."

"Not Amy," he repeats, low and soft as he cautiously approaches.

"Not Amy."

"Not Amy," he says again.

"Not anymore."

"Not to me." He slowly settles down on the bed beside me. "You've never been Amy. You are Alaska. Always have been. Always will be."

"Arizona gave me that name," I explain, sounding rushed and frenzied even in my ears. "It was to help me start over. I don't know why I said Amy." I shake my head hard. "I don't want to be Amy. I'm Alaska."

"You're Alaska." His voice drops to a lower decibel, and I feel his lips press against my hair. "You're my Alaska. My beautiful, brave, strong, and determined Alaska."

Also, foolish? Stupid? The voice says in my head, but I don't dare the say words out loud. Not when he's so kind and patient with me. He's not like this often. And honestly, I'm not this shaken too often. But it's happening more lately. The more I open up, the more I'm feeling lost and jittery. I don't know what can fix it.

Maybe Taylis is the cause. Perhaps I can't be surrounded by kindness and patience.

Maybe I'm one of those people who can only thrive under a rough hand and sharp words.

The idea makes me sad.

"Relax, Alaska," Taylis continues in that soothing, warm voice. I turn into jelly when he's soft like this. But I hate that I also feel weak. Not even two years on Hethdiss and I'm allowing myself to be weak around clients. I can't be weak around them. Clients are supposed to fuck me, not comfort me.

There's only one thing I can do to help get myself get into the right mindset of a Call-Girl again.

CHAPTER 9

TAYLIS

Scheita, I am a weak male. A very weak male. I know something is wrong. Every bone and scale in my body screams that something is wrong but that all gets pushed to the side when Alaska slips her hand inside my shorts and grabs my cock.

"No," I mutter, pinching my eyes shut as the shame of being twisted once again by this alien female washes over me. She doesn't know how much power she has over me. "We need to talk, Alaska. What did you think about? Did you have another terror?"

"I don't want to talk." At least she sounds like she's telling the truth, but it's hard to tell when she's stroking up and down my length. I groan loudly. "Taylis, I need to stop thinking so much about my past and focus more on my present." She circles her finger around the head of my cock, gathering a few beads of precum that have already gathered. "Wouldn't you rather fuck your human female?"

"You are my Chosen mate," I say, barely managing to keep control.

"I'm yours. You own me," she purrs, leaning down against my ear. "What do words matter, anyway? Pleasure mate? Chosen mate? Human whore? They're all the same."

"They are not," I insist.

"They are," she hisses back, squeezing my crown. "They all mean you own me. You can use me as you want. You can take me when you please. Why can't we return to that? Why does it have to be so personal?"

"I thought you wanted personal," I say, taking in a sharp breath to calm myself.

"Not if it's going to be so painful."

"I can help you, Alaska. I can—"

"Stop." I jerk suddenly, blinking and looking down to see Alaska quickly removing my shorts. Her eyes flick up to mine. "Wouldn't you rather me suck your dick for a little while?" To prove her point, she leans down and blows cold air over the tip. "Isn't this better than talking about the past?"

"It's better." I can't help admitting, trying to move away from her searching mouth. But I'm helpless when her tongue brushes down at the root. "Scheita, Alaska. It's better. I admit that."

"I know it is. What male doesn't want his cock sucked?" She flicks her tongue again before kissing my tip, sucking gently. I can't lose focus. I'm trying so hard, but she's good. Way too good at what she does. "Since when do you want to talk about my past? Or anyone's past at all?" she purrs.

"Because it's you."

"Uh-huh. Because I'm an alien, right?"

"You are an alien," I can't help admitting, fisting the nearest pile of sheets as she takes my entire cock between her lips. "That's fine. You said I am an alien to you. We are both aliens, yes?"

She shakes her head with me still in her mouth before pulling away, leaving me breathless. "But it's different because you are a big, bad, blue male, yes? You have to protect females. You have to dominate them. That's what Sidyths want."

"We're here because we *don't* want that."

"*Some* don't," she grumbles, cupping my sack, and stars burst in my vision as she kneads them carefully. "I think you do. I think you don't want an alien mate because you want someone weak and easy to dominate."

"No," I gasp, trying to reach for her, but she ducks her head, retaking me into her mouth and sucking hard. "Ahhh… scheita!"

"You Sidyths pretend you're so much better than your brothers back on your homeworld. Maybe even the supposed *outsiders*. Well, at least they're honest with themselves. Honest about who they are." She bobs her head and sucks me hard from root to tip, dragging her teeth along the delicate skin. I'm helpless to argue with her, even as she continues to speak between sucks. I'm too out of breath between attentions. "They will at least admit that they think alien females are weak. Alien human females. They wouldn't lie to make themselves look good. They wouldn't say they care and then talk shit about them behind their back. No. They'd fuck and move on. It's easier that way."

My eyes pop open despite me feeling the need to come. *Focus, Taylis, focus!* "What are you talking about—"

"Those assholes wouldn't make me feel like it's okay to be vulnerable only to speak to their brothers. Calling her foolish. Stupid, even."

I try rising on my elbows. "Wait… I didn't—ah, no!"

"Yes," she hisses across my dick. "I know what you said. I heard you. You called me foolish."

"I didn't. Alaska. Stop. *Stop this now!*"

The authority in my voice must have registered as a command because suddenly, Alaska's soft, moist lips are no longer wrapped around my cock. It's painful to be so close to release and not get there, but there are more important things to deal with. I sit up in bed, flashing Alaska with my firmest glare.

"That is enough. *What were you talking about earlier?"* She lowers her eyes, avoiding my gaze. That's better. At least she's more like herself now. Less crazed. Less wild. I can handle her this way. And though I don't like being so dominant with her, I don't know what else to do. She's good at using pleasure to distract me. I have a feeling all the females are.

"I heard them." Alaska's voice is like a wisp of wind across the humid space between us.

"Heard who? Heard what?" Now that I feel back in control and my cock is no longer throbbing for release, I grab Alaska and place her down on her back on the bed and look down at her. Her breasts are heaving, glistening with sweat as she breathes at a rapid pace as I hover over her, and though this probably isn't easy for her, she needs to know that just because I can dominate her physically, doesn't mean that I will ever hurt her. "Tell me what you heard, Alaska."

She doesn't hesitate. "Cade. Dash. One of them."

I arch an eyebrow. "What did they say?"

"They called me foolish. Stupid."

Red dots of anger flash before me. "They did. I'll challenge them. I'll—"

"They said they talked to *you*," she hisses. "Did you say that to them? Did you call me foolish? Stupid?"

"No."

"Did you tell them what happened in the woods? That I ran away from you?"

I blink. "I… yes. But I didn't…" I trail off, trying to remember my exact words. I was frustrated at the time. I might have let something slip. I might have said… "I don't remember exactly what I said to them." Her lower lip trembles, and I lean closer to her face. "But you must know I don't feel that way. Not anymore. Not about you."

Her expression shifts. "How do you feel about me then? Honest and truly?"

"Honest and truly? Is that a human term of some sort?"

"A weak, female term, sure."

"Stop that," I hiss. "I don't know what I said, but you are not a weak female. Have I not told you already?"

"Tell me again." I notice a change in the air. More importantly, a change in her scent. "I've told you how I feel. I want to hear from you."

"Very well." I lower my body, making sure my lips are dangerously close to her ears so she will not only hear my words but feel them as well. "I think you changed how I felt about Choosing an alien for a mate." I flick my tongue across her earlobe, and she moans, bucking her hips violently. *Well, this is certainly a nice change.* "I think that despite my worries about taking an alien for a mate, you are so much more than that. You are not just an alien. You are not just a human. You are Alaska. And Alaska is the one I want."

She stiffens beneath me, and though I'm probably taking a significant risk, I can't help myself and use my hand to cup one of her round, soft teets and squeeze it gently.

"Ohh… Taylis," she murmurs, pressing her body up into mine.

"Is that what you want to hear?"

"I want you to take me."

My eyes widen, but I am too weak to ask questions. Her entire demeanor has changed, and though I'm sure it's because she thinks I'm using her the way I want, that's not it. I'm giving this female precisely what she needs. A male who respects her. A male who will make her cry out in ecstasy. A male who enjoys not only every soft curve of her body but who also wants to soothe every painful memory. She's never had a male in her life like me before. I intend to make sure no other male will ever have the chance.

It only takes a few moments before we're both naked and I've got her legs dragged over the edge of the bed as I crouch on the floor before her. The pink folds of her pussy glisten with arousal, and her beautiful bud is throbbing – practically begging for my attention. I lean forward and sniff around the curls covering her slit, remembering how good she is down here. Spicy and sweet. Like the most exquisite dessert after a warm meal on a chilly day. Goddess, how I want this. Want her.

I grip her thighs, rising to give myself leverage. Alaska watches me with a curious expression. "You sure know how to get ready for me, don't you?"

"I can't help it," she says in a low voice. "My body belongs to you."

"If that's the case, then my body belongs to you, as well."

"That's not—"

Not wanting to get into another argument, I press my tongue against her opening, enjoying her throaty little cry out. "If your body belongs to me, my body belongs to you," I say, insisting. *"My body belongs to you. But your body belongs to me. Say it, Alaska."*

She hesitates, trying to push her pussy towards my cock, but I'm not about to be distracted this time.

"Say it to me."

"My body belongs to you. Your body belongs to me."

Her words still sound hesitant, but I can only be so strong. The scent of her cunt is almost too much to handle. Her spicy, sweet scent is thick in the air, so much so I can taste it on my tongue. I shift my mouth away from her cunt. It's not enough. I need to be inside her now. In a quick movement, I'm on top of her once again, teasing the wet folds of her pussy with my cock, watching as she grows more and more desperate for my touch. For me.

"Do you want this?" I ask in a low voice.

"Yes."

"Then repeat it." She frowns up at me. *"Say it.* I'll never get tired of hearing it, and I want you to learn to love it. Because it's true. Repeat it."

"My body belongs to you."

"And?"

"Your body belongs to me."

"That's good. And now… I'm going to penetrate you. Is that what you want?"

"More than anything."

Her eyes roll into the back of her head as I push my cock through her opening, and her pussy gives me a little welcome hug as a hello. I want to make sure every nook and cranny of her sweet cunt is filled because her body truly does belong to me. And mine to her. I push deep inside until I bottom out, and for a few moments, I merely just let my cock rest there. Bobbing inside.

"Taylis—"

"Say you want more. *Say it to me."*

"I want more, Taylis. God, I need you—"

I pull out only to thrust back deeply inside her. I use my hand to seek out her throbbing clit, adding to her pleasure. I know I'm hard on her, but she needs to know that despite who's in charge, we're in this together. I want her to come. I want to come as well. It's all about mutual release. That's what it's got to all be about. I pinch her clit, and she bucks upward, her head nearly colliding with mine.

"You needed this," I hiss "Very badly."

She nods wordlessly, taking the pounding I'm giving her without being gentle. Alaska wouldn't want it that way anyway. I can be gentle with her if there's another time. If that's what she wants. And there will be another time. But not now. This fucking isn't about showing how sweet I can be. It's about showing that I want her. Not just in name, but in every sense. I don't want a pleasure mate. I don't want a Chosen mate. None of those words matter! I just want her. Alaska…

"My Alaska."

"Say it again."

"You are my Alaska."

She stiffens, and her blunt little nails drag across my back, attempting to break the skin. She cries out when her orgasm washes over her, and her cunt gives me another tight hug that sends me toppling over the edge of my climax as well. I don't pull out, filling her with everything I've got because she can't get pregnant anyway. I want her to feel me. She's felt my come before, sure, but this fuck session is so different than the others. It's warmer. More welcoming. Hotter. Searing—

"God, you're so cold!" she yells, squirming around beneath me and around my cock. I can't help smiling. I suppose that just because it's hot for me doesn't mean my release feels any less chilly to her.

I pull my hand away from her clit, allowing her breathing to settle, and roll off to the side beside her in bed, staring up at the ceiling.

"*Mine.*" Without hesitating, I reach across the bed and pull her soft, sweaty body up against mine, and kiss her hair.

"Yours."

I like the sound of that.

CHAPTER 10

ALASKA

THE FOLLOWING MORNING, **I** WANT TO TELL MYSELF THAT **I**'M **at ease with everything that happened.** Taylis doesn't think I'm just some simple, foolish female, and I must admit it feels damn good.

Even looking at him now, slumbering loudly after a particularly rough fuck makes me smile. I never had an issue with physical attraction when it comes to Taylis. Yeah, some aliens are weird as hell to look at, but Sidyths are pretty humanoid – save for the blue skin, scales, and claws. Oh, and not to mention the average height of their males' hovers around seven feet tall. Despite those differences, I was drawn to Taylis. Even if I didn't understand it at the time, he could have treated me like a paid-by-the-hour slut the moment he brought me to his lair, but he didn't bother.

Maybe he always knew I had problems.

Ugh. Problems. They still exist. And yes, it's great that I can temporarily forget about them when Taylis is running his hands all over my body and thrusting his impressive dick inside me, but something still doesn't feel quite right.

Am I ready to give up working as an Intergalactic Call-Girl?

What if things don't work out?

There are already whisperings that this little utopia Prince Korben's built may not last forever. What happens then? My motto has always been not to chase happiness because it will hurt more when it's taken away.

But now I'm wondering, is that any way to live?

I take in a deep sigh, and release it slowly, hating that I'm searching for reasons to escape. Who wants to be a space whore? Who wants to spread their legs for aliens? Even if I did somehow manage to leave this assignment with my heart intact, who's to say Arizona would come? Dakota? Kansas? What if we split up? It's happened before… it could just as quickly occur again. I can't turn that feeling of unease off like a light switch. I can't put so much faith into something and someone that may not be guaranteed. The sex is great, but it doesn't change anything. Not really.

Taylis is still an alien. He's still a Sidyth with an entire world and history waiting for him on his home planet. I don't know anything about his family life or his friends or his upbringing. He keeps talking about my past, but he's never really shared any of his with me. And maybe that's because he misses it. He must want to go home. And what would happen to me if he did? What if the next delivery guy says Prince Korben's father has forgiven him and all Sidyths who wish to return home, could?

Shaking my head, I stand and pull on my skirt and top as quietly as I can, so I don't wake up Taylis. I can't face him right now. Not yet. He thinks everything has changed now, and whatever. But in the morning hours, I'm not entirely sure I'm ready to risk it all on a chance he'll want to stay with me after he's allowed to return home.

I shouldn't tease myself with the idea of a happily ever after. Arizona would have never allowed it. She practically slapped Kansas over an alien client she had a few cycles before this assignment. Now she has a mate. A real mate. And she's so convinced we're all going to live here. But she can't know that. No one can. Not really. And though Taylis says sweet words and makes me come, it doesn't mean he'll stay in exile when he can return to his homeworld.

I don't want this to be so difficult. I hate thinking on my own. I never trust myself. My stepfather's friends told me what to do, and I did it. My stepfather told me I was worthless and had nowhere else to go, and I believed him. And when Brady's cousin took me away from school to sign some paper, I did it because I didn't want to find out what would happen if I didn't… only to have to sign the dotted line anyway. I like being ordered around. It keeps me from thinking or dealing with any responsibility. That's why I liked Arizona so much. Why I still do. I trust her judgments more than I trust my own.

But what is my judgment?

Thinking about it… if I didn't have Arizona to think about. Or Dakota. Or Kansas. Or Washington. Or even Taylis? What would I want? To risk it all? To stay on Hethdiss and see if Taylis and I really can stay here forever and start a family? Trust he won't leave my side? Trust he'll fight to keep me by his side? Forever? Last night, I would have said yes. He wanted me so much I could feel it in every thrust.

But what about tomorrow? And the next day? Another year? Five? Ten? When I'm going grey and getting wrinkly, will Taylis still want me? Do Sidyths age the same as humans? Will he want to upgrade when I'm no longer as young and hot? Will I wake up one day and he'll be gone… back to his homeworld to get a real mate of his own kind? I hate that I don't know for sure. I hate that my answer could change from moment to moment. I hate having to make any decision entirely on my own.

Deciding to take a break from the secondary lair in general, I stroll across the fields between that and the central den. It's surprisingly quiet, but I guess it's still early in the morning, so that's all right. I enjoy the quiet. After long nights, especially on tougher assignments, I'd love coming back to my room with the girls. Some would be with clients, but I would rarely find myself alone.

I loved coming back and seeing Arizona or Dakota waiting there for me. They'd lift their chins, give me tired smiles and pat a spot on the floor. Our housing situations weren't always the best when we didn't have to stay with clients all night, but I never minded, so long as I got to be with one of my girls – even if we spent the entire time sitting in silence.

When I'm finally at the central lair opening, something makes me hesitate, even when Ellis lifts her head. She's seated on the floor with her monster of a toddler-baby-man beside her and her mate, Hujun, is nowhere in sight.

"Hey," she greets me. "You don't usually come out this way."

I spare her a smile. "Just needed to get out and take a walk."

"I get it." She juts a thumb over her shoulder. "I think some of the girls are already awake and in the Gathering Room. Hujun just went to grab me some breakfast."

"Gotcha," I say awkwardly. The idea of being around some of the other girls stresses me out, so I back away slowly. "Well, I think I'm just going to go around for a walk."

"Sounds good. Remember we're on high alert."

"Right."

I'm not paying close attention to her words because I'm

scrambling to get away as I detect more voices from deeper inside the central lair. Seeing happy couples and babies is probably the last thing I need. It could all end tomorrow; I keep telling myself. Really. It could all end tomorrow and—

My thoughts come to a grinding halt when a strange sound prickles the edge of my hearing. It almost sounds like… *no*. That wouldn't be right. I glance over my shoulder.

"Hey," I call back to Ellis. "Are the workout twins out today?"

She shakes her head. "Already done."

I turn away without saying anything else, convinced the sound I heard must have been a mistake.

Because for a moment it sounded like a female. But that can't be right.

Still though, with nothing else to do, I head further away from the lairs, enjoying the muggy air after what must have been a night of heavy rainfall. Usually, I notice these kinds of things, but the sex I had last night must have been particularly loud because I didn't hear a damn thing.

When I get close to the borders, I narrow my eyes into the distance and try listening more carefully. I hear those monkey beast things, but not much else. A large cluster of trees looms to the right, and the monkey beast territory is straight ahead. Yeah, I won't be heading that way. This world is strangely beautiful when I give myself a chance to appreciate it. Surely it wouldn't be terrible to live here. I take a step beyond the tree line, officially crossing over the borders set by Prince Korben and Hujun when the same voice that sent prickles up my spine sounds off again. There's no mistaking it now. Away from the hood of the trees, it does sound like a woman.

A human.

How's that possible, though? Ellis said Devyn and Rene already finished their morning run. The fields were empty when I crossed between lairs, and I'm sure Ellis would have mentioned something about anyone out. I guess. I think. Squinting, I try to figure out exactly where the sound comes from, and thankfully, the cries don't seem to be coming from the monkey beast territory or the looming dark purple trees. I glance to the left, trying to remember what's in that direction, but all I can think about is Sloane's anti-social mate. I think he goes that way when he wants to get away from others.

Maybe it's Sloane and her mate trying out a little BDSM in the morning hours?

Another cry fills the air, and instinctively I realize that whatever, or whoever is making that sound, doesn't seem to be enjoying themselves. I should go back. Go back to the lair and tell Ellis what's going on, and she can tell her man to check on this. That would make the most sense.

But I think harder.

The Sidyths think we're weak. Vulnerable.

How stupid would they all look if one of their females got lost and they didn't even notice? How stupid would they look if another female brought her back safe and sound? Cade and Dash wouldn't dare call me foolish or weak then. And then Taylis wouldn't just have to *say* I'm strong or brave. He would know it for a fact. I take a hesitant step in the direction of the cries.

Is this a good idea? The lairs are on high alert. The smart thing to do would be to head back and tell someone. Don't be foolish.

I'm not even sure what voice I'm hearing in my head right now, but at this point, I don't even think it matters. All my life, I've done what others have told me. I've been told how to sit, who to sit with, when to keep quiet, and when to sign a dotted line. I've been ordered to fuck aliens who made me want to barf. I've spread when I just wanted to cry for my mom. And now, for the first time in my life, I have the chance to do something I want to do even if it is stupid. Even if it is foolish.

It's a bad idea.

"Fuck off," I tell the voice in my head. No one's going to tell me what to do this time.

I may be doing something stupid or dangerous.

But at least I can say I did it all on my own.

CHAPTER 11

TAYLIS

ALASKA IS NOT IN OUR BED WHEN I WAKE. IT SHOULDN'T ALARM me as much as it does, but something about the taste of the air puts me on high alert. I waste no time, retrieving my shorts and striding to the Gathering Room, but not surprisingly, Alaska is not there. Hardly any of the females glance in my direction, and though Drozass spots me and saunters over, I'm already moving.

Something is wrong.

I stop in front of the lair opening and glance out, checking for her scent, and though it is there, it is faint across the humid skies. Besides, it is difficult to focus now that Drozass has come up behind me and is filling my nostrils with the scent of his and his mate's pleasure.

"What is wrong?" Drozass has always been like this. He goes straight to the point. I suppose that's a good quality in a moment like this.

"My mate," I say thickly. "She was not in bed when I woke."

Drozass frowns deeply. "Did she have plans to do anything? Perhaps she went to visit one of her companions. My Arizona—"

"Her scent is already faint." I dart my tongue from my lips. "Almost as though it is being covered somehow."

His frown deepens. "That does not mean she is in danger. What happened to Arizona will not happen to her."

"How can you be sure?" I hiss. "We spoke on this. The *outsiders* grow more curious. The wilder ones more interested. Delivery comes soon. We know they want more females. What better way to explain what they want than to show them an example?" I cross my arms across my chest, fighting the urge to sprint across the fields in the direction of her fading scent. "I fear Alaska is still haunted by her past. She spoke of leaving me before to be with *outsiders*."

"*She what?*" Drozass' horrified look sends a wave of shame down my spine. "Is it true, brother? Does she truly wish to run from you rather than share her past?"

"I don't know anymore," I hiss, frustrated, and embarrassed that it seems I cannot control my female.

"Taylis…" Drozass trails off, staring off into the talas where Alaska must have run to get away from me. Nothing else makes sense. Is it possible? Is it as I fear? Did Alaska only use pleasure to distract me? To prove I am no different? The thought leaves me frustrated, but Drozass speaks before my thoughts grow more frenzied. "You must be reasonable, brother. These females… these who have been working for a long time… they have a difficult time understanding kindness. My Arizona was the same—"

"It is not the same," I hiss. "Your mate was tricked. My mate left me."

"We do not know that for sure, brother." He drapes a hand across my shoulders, and though I stiffen under his touch, I admit is has a momentarily calming effect. "Though the lairs are on high alert, I am sure she did not go far. She is a smart female."

"She ran from me," I say under my breath, shaking my head in disbelief. "She mentioned things would be better if she were misused. Maybe she meant what she said."

Drozass frowns. "I refuse to believe that. Her place is here with us, and her female companions. And with you, Taylis."

"That is what I thought too, brother, but how can I believe it now? I thought I was getting through to her. I thought that perhaps telling me about her past would help. But it seems to have had the opposite effect. She only ran further this time."

"She may return—"

"Or maybe she ran right into the arms of an outsider for real this time," I hiss. "Maybe that's what she wanted the entire time. Maybe she never wanted to be with me. And I can't say I blame her. Brother, I must admit something to you."

"Oh? What is it?"

I lower my head. "When I initially requested that Alaska and become Chosen mates… it was in name only."

Drozass sucks in a breath. "You… you did what? What does this mean? In name only?"

"If anyone would ask of us, we were Chosen mates… but in privacy… we remained pleasure mates."

"Why would you do this?" I feel the disgust radiating off his tongue in waves. "Why would you do that to a female? Did she request this?"

"I thought that's what she wanted. I was wrong. She wanted to be true Chosen mates."

"Did you?"

I consider his question seriously. Yes, I've said I've wanted to be Chosen mates in passing, but have I meant it? Have I considered all the consequences? Never returning home? Drozass may not care because he has nothing to return to, but I am tothid on the fatherland. I come from a wealthy line and proud heritage. I would never be welcomed back with an alien by my side. And the idea left me so disgusted anyway. Humans are so fragile. So frail. Emotional. Weak. Alien. But Alaska always surprised me. She wasn't always fragile. She was never emotional. The only time she acted that way was when—

"She trusted me," I mutter under my breath, stepping out into the fields. Drozass is quick to follow.

"That's not an answer," Drozass calls, falling in step beside me. "Do not chase after the female if you do not want her. Allow someone else to track her down if there is even something to be worried about."

"There is something to be worried about," I hiss in a low voice, gazing outward. "I know there is. Alaska wouldn't... she wouldn't have just run off."

"But you said—"

"I know what I said. But I also know Alaska. And something is wrong. I feel it." I thump my fist against my chest. "I feel it here. Something is not right."

Without allowing another moment for Alaska's scent to fade, I break out into a sprint across the fields. Drozass calls for me, but I can't waste any time looking back. I've lost so much time already.

At the border, I dart my tongue from my lips, desperate to see if anything has changed in her scent. But it is as it was. It's being covered. Worry for my mate prickles up my spine. I need to figure out a direction she could be.

I dart my attention to the dilewiler territory, and yet I find the scent even more faded. I want to believe Alaska would not head this way. I sniff around Exer's territory, and nothing catches my attention. Ugh! I hate how this takes so much time! I know it makes sense to stay focused and take time tracking her down, but I don't know how long she's been gone. Or if she's genuinely in any danger. Maybe Drozass is right. Maybe she needed time away from me — time to think.

Or maybe it is as Alaska said and there's no other way she can exist without being ordered around.

Why couldn't she have spoken to me about it? Why did she have to disappear without a word? I would have listened. If talk about her past was too overwhelming, I would have dropped the subject entirely if that's what she wanted. I have all but offered that already. But I also kept questioning – convinced I would be the solution to her problems. It was arrogant on my part, and if I somehow find Alaska, I will let her know I was in the wrong. I will apologize with both hearts and hope to the Goddess that she will forgive me. I can only hope if something did happen to her, that I don't arrive too late.

Deciding to head in the opposite direction of Exer's territory, I hope I'm making the right decision. Her scent is slightly headier this way, though I can't pick up on any emotions. That's Alaska, all right. So difficult. Even if she's afraid, even her scent won't always tell me so. She is a frustrating female. I shouldn't want her. She is alien. She may not even want me after all of this.

But I can't stop running. It is my fault she left. It is my fault she did not feel comfortable enough speaking to me about her past or worries. She runs into the arms of cruelty rather than deal with someone who wants to be kind to her. I stop in my tracks, wafting the air with my hand to have a better taste around me, but the scent of Alaska fades once again. No, I can't lose track of her. I'm sure she's around here somewhere!

Despite the fading scent, I push ahead because I'm not sure what else to do. I don't know or care if Drozass or any of my brothers are following me or trying to help me track down a missing female. None of it matters. I must find her. No matter what she wants, I need to see her one more time. I need her to look me in the eyes and state directly that she does not want me.

If she can say that to me, I will be done with her. No matter what. I will not force a female to be with me. No matter how much it would hurt.

That's when I catch it — the sweet, spicy mix of Alaska's scent. I stop in my tracks, head darting around to figure out the sudden change. It is not much here. The Great Cliff is in the distance, but I didn't imagine it. Alaska was here. And whatever is trying to mask her scent, obviously missed a spot, because I can taste her so directly that she may as well stand before me.

Sweet and spicy, just like the female it belongs to. She was here. I feel that now, and though I'm getting ready to start sprinting again, something makes me hesitate.

Not alone.

I inhale deeply, scales splaying from my skin as the realization washes over. Whatever happened here... Alaska was not alone. There are other scents. Two distinctive scents. Two males. Sidyth. *Outsiders.* I drop to a crouch and brush my claws over the dirt and grass, not surprised to find it flattened. A struggle. Maybe a fight. Luckily, I don't smell anything sexual, but I don't feel fear either, which worries me. Did she come out here to meet with two other males? Was this planned? Had she expected to leave me this whole time? The idea makes me snarl under my breath.

What is going on? It's so hard to tell what happened here, but I should focus on what's important. Alaska was here. And now that I've picked up on her, I can tell which direction she headed in. With two other males. *Why?*

I know it's a bad idea for me to find out. For all I know, Alaska met with males this entire time, and now that she sees me as no different than the other males in her life, she's decided to leave the lairs entirely. But something about that conclusion doesn't sit right. Alaska is frustrating, but she isn't cruel. She wouldn't have done this to me. She couldn't have done this to me.

I rise back up to my full height and continue in the direction that Alaska's scent fades once more. I have no idea what I'm going to see when I find her. I'm not even sure if I'm even going to want to see what's happening. But I must know. I heard the little mewling sounds pouring from my mate's throat. It didn't feel like an act. It didn't feel like a trick. It felt like a female who was beginning to accept that the male who's Chosen her... may be the perfect mate.

I shouldn't think about pleasuring Alaska. It only makes my cock stiffen, and I need to be able to move quickly. I break out into a sprint, allowing my feet to pound heavily on the earth while constantly darting my tongue out to keep track of her and the two males who are now mixing their scents with my Alaska.

Mine.

The hills rise as I grow closer to the Great Cliff, and there are plenty of hidden valleys behind the talas. It would be easy enough to get trapped in one of those things. This place is like a maze. Take a wrong turn, and practically run right into a collection of dirt. There is no escape if someone is tracking you down. I make sure to keep myself on high alert, not wanting to end up trapped in one of these valleys, just in case I'm not alone in my search for Alaska.

It's still early, so the suns are only still beginning to rise, but the air now is growing warmer and muggier. I'm thankful it is not raining today. Otherwise, this chase would prove even more difficult than it already is. Already it feels like my lungs are burning, but I won't stop running.

Even if I don't like what I see at the end of this trip, I must see it with my own eyes.

I must know if Alaska has denied me. Even if it kills me, I need to hear her say the words.

She has to say she does not want me.

But if something has happened to her? If these other two males are with my Alaska, and she did not wish it so? That will be a problem.

I pick up the pace, hoping I'm not on a fool's errand. But just as I'm about to doubt myself even further, I swear I hear a voice crying in the distance.

Alaska's voice.

I sprint harder. *I must know what this is all about.*

CHAPTER 12

ALASKA

I SHOULDN'T HAVE GONE AFTER THAT VOICE. I BELIEVED I WAS
going to do something great. Something that would prove to so
many others, Sidyths especially, that humans aren't some weak,
primitive race. We can do things. We can feel things. We are
strong.

But I haven't found the owner of the cries. Whatever's
making the noise only grows further away as I struggle to keep up
with it.

I don't even know where I am now. I stop and glance around,
trying to remember the way I came, but just as I'm about to run, I
hear it again.

The cry for help.

The voice sounds so scared and frightened, but I don't understand how it keeps moving further and further away. I've been
jogging for a while now, and I don't feel any closer than I did
when I started.

I'm worried that Taylis is going to think I ran away from. And he would be entirely in his right to think so. I had sex with him. He probably thought things went well, and then BOOM, the next morning, I'm gone. Oh God, it looks terrible. It seems so freaking bad.

And now I'm not sure if it makes more sense to keep sprinting after the voice or try finding my way back to the lairs.

Stopping for a moment, I glance up at the hot pink suns blazing overhead, guessing that if I were back on Earth, it'd be around ten or eleven in the morning. The temperature only continues to rise. It's muggy, and suddenly I'm missing the cold, damp air of the underground lairs. Even more importantly, I'm missing a blue, scaled alien who always manages to make me think cruelty isn't my only option in life.

I wonder if he's even looking for me now. He probably thinks I'm off being a bitch and giving me time to think. What reason should he have to look for me?

Because I'm his Chosen mate? I don't even know what we are anymore! Chosen mates for real, or Chosen mates in name? Does he want me? Do I want him? *Yes, of course you do, Alaska. Don't be stupid.* The little voice of reason in my head makes me gasp out. It's true. I do want him. I want to try. Why am I only realizing this while I'm running around the woods of an alien planet when the temperature is approaching one hundred degrees in the late morning?

"Fuck..." I grumble, pushing a hand through my hair and finding a way to use some of it to create a ponytail with the rest. I'm hot. Really hot.

I shouldn't think about it. My focus either needs to be getting back to the lair and Taylis or trying to find this woman crying out for me.

I know what makes more sense. But I've come this far. Might as well see it through to the end.

I push aside some heavy branches of the trees hanging high over my head. I can't get over the sight of them. They smell like Christmas trees but shaped like palm trees, and the trunks are a dark purple, and the leaves are light purple. It's jarring, especially against the teal grass and blue dirt, but I can't even appreciate that right now.

Because there comes that voice, that cry out for help.

I can't give up. Not when I've come this far.

For too long, I've allowed others to call the shots just because it was easier. Fighting never changed anything. My stepfather. Brady. Arizona. Alien clients. It was always easier to do what they wanted. Fighting brought problems. Tanner made sure I followed orders from an early age, and I have to say, up until I arrived on Hethdiss, I was happy with the way things were going. Or, maybe happy isn't the right word. I wasn't unhappy.

You were dead inside, Alaska. Taylis is the first being who's made you feel alive.

I should be happy about that. My brain is finally rebelling against me. But how can I feel happy when I have no one to share the news with? Taylis isn't here. Arizona's been telling me to take control of my life for a while. I'm only just realizing that Taylis, even if our happiness is only temporary, is who I want right now, what I need.

Damnit. I should have told him. Should have let him know that he makes me feel alive like no one else ever did anymore.

Instead, I'm chasing after some voice crying out for me in the woods of an alien planet. That makes sense.

I glance back over my shoulder mid-run, wondering if I should turn around and head back in the opposite direction. I'm bound to see something familiar. Some indication that I'm heading back to the lairs. No. Not just the lairs. I'd be heading back home. My home.

But something makes me hesitate. Not only the crying ahead

of me but the rustling. I've noticed it since I left the lairs boundaries, but I assumed it had something to do with the voice calling out. But it's coming from another direction. Instead of ahead of me, this sound comes from my right. I don't like it. The movements are sloppy; reminding me more of how a large animal would sound crushing through the woods than stealthy beings like the Sidyths.

I shouldn't think about that. So long as I stay ahead, I should be all right. If I turned around now, whatever's following me on the right, would be able to catch me with ease.

Don't think about it, Alaska. Just go. Go somewhere. Don't stand still.

I'm about to take a step when the rustling crunches to my right grow impossibly close, and the trees break apart. I stagger backward, unsure of what's coming. I reach around blindly for a fallen branch in the grass, but of course, I come up empty-handed. I freeze in place as a flash of white catches my eyes, and fear of the unknown leaves me about to piss my pants.

It's… it's a… I don't even know how to describe it.

There are eight long, spindly legs like a spider. But there are also two arms. It has a white body… but it's fuzzy like a cotton ball or serving of cotton candy. And the white is… splattered with red. *Blood.* It's also not the size of a normal spider. Its fuzzy white body is the size of a rubber ball from gym class that we used to play a game called 'four-square,' and if it rose upon those eight legs, it would be taller than a Sidyth. It has two brilliantly large red eyes glaring right at me, but it's not moving. Now that we're in each other's eyesight, it seems to be almost as alarmed as I am.

That could work for, or completely against me as far as I'm concerned.

The blood all over its body leans toward working against me.

"Nice… uh… doggy?" I try, hoping my voice is soft and

soothing enough that the creature won't feel the need to attack. Maybe it's just curious about me.

The white, fuzzy spider does the last thing I want though, and rises on those eight legs, almost as though to remind both of us that he's the larger one. I take a shaky step backward, trying to convince myself that running away would be a bad idea, but it's hard to take me seriously when I can see the fangs of this alien creature are the size of my wrist and tipped with fresh blood.

We've appeared to reach a standoff, and not coming up with any other ideas, I crouch, spreading out my arms and legs in hopes of making myself look as wide as possible. This creature has the height, but maybe if I can trick it into thinking I've got the weight, he'll leave me alone.

A strange rasping sound escapes his mouth (wherever that is), and bats one of its shorter arm things in my direction. I jump back.

"No!" The command leaves my throat without permission, and I'm worried I've signed my death certificate. But the creature's short arm draws back, and he lowers himself slowly by bending his long legs. He reaches out a second time. "I said, no!" And it draws away. *It's listening to me.* This strange creature thing is listening to me! I want to be excited about it, but I'm not out of the woods yet. Just because it's not touching me, doesn't mean it's not going to eat me.

And that's when I hear another sound. A similar sound. This time coming from behind me. I spin around, and sure enough, there's another fuzzy, spider thing. And it's not slow-moving. It's also double the size of the one I'm dealing with now.

Okay, time for animal training is over.

Spinning away from both creatures, I break out into a sprint, no longer caring what direction I'm heading. I need to get away. I hear the spiders behind me — all ten of their respective legs pounding on the earth and through the branches. I'm already tired from running after an unknown voice, but now I'm running from something so somehow, I manage to get my second wind.

Giant, white puffy ball spider things are chasing me through the woods. No one will believe it. That is, no one will believe it if I manage to get out of this mess alive. I'm so scared I want to cry, but the spiders won't even allow me the liberty, picking up the pace in their pursuit and making more of those horrible screeching sounds that are way too much like nails on a chalkboard.

Got to keep running. I can't possibly fight these things. They're bigger than me.

And bloody. So bloody.

The temperature is scorching, though, and the human body isn't designed for heavy sprinting in dense humidity. I'm going to run out of steam, and then I'll be nothing but easy pickings for these monsters.

No. I'm going to get out of this. As I keep dashing, I look for a spot to dart to the left or right, hoping to trick the monsters, but no such luck. Most of the turns are dead ends. As in, if I turned in there, my life would end, and I'd be dead. Nope, there's nowhere left to go onward and—*upward.*

The word hits me so violently that I nearly stumble, ending my attempt to survive before I even begin. I lift my eyes on the trees, trying to check if there's a place. Just one place. Only one piece of bark I can jump onto and hope to holly hell that –
THERE IT IS!

Relief pounds through my temples as I notice a tree maybe twenty yards ahead that may work. I'll have to push myself harder than I've ever pushed before, but if I can do this, I may have a chance to survive. Letting out a fear cry to push my body to the limits, I jump at the trunk when I reach the base, curling my fingers around the shelf-like feature of the trunk and hurl myself up. My upper-body strength isn't anything like the workout twins, but it does the trick. I'm able to pull myself up. And again. And then again, until I'm about twelve feet in the air and looking down as the more massive beast crashes headfirst into the tree.

It wasn't an accident. He tried throwing me out.

Which mean… he can't climb.

"You can't climb!" I screech, panting and sweating more than I've ever done in my life. "You can't get me, motherfucker!" My sweaty fingers loosen around the branch I'm holding onto, but nothing, NOTHING, is going to make me fall from this tree. Not now. I'm triumphant. "You thought you could get me! You were wrong, fuckers!"

The beasts screech and hiss at me, and though I'm dying to cover my ears, I won't. I won't lose focus. I need to make sure I'm right and that these creatures won't suddenly crawl up after me like an ant. It only takes a few moments for me to realize they can't. They try, but their legs aren't strong enough to support their weight, and they don't have fingers at the end of their spindly legs and arms to curl into the bark to hold their weight.

I'm safe. Only temporarily, but I'm safe.

"Can anybody hear me?" I shout, hoping I'm not asking for more trouble, but unless these creatures leave, I'm kind of up shit's creek without a paddle here. They don't seem to be losing interest, and occasionally, the larger one rams his body against the trunk trying to shake me loose from my spot. I grip the branch more tightly and look down.

Still only two. But for how long? There's got to be more of these things around here, and do I want to be stuck in a tree when they arrive? What if these are just the babies? What does a mamma spider beast look like? Will she be big enough to pluck me from the tree while standing? I swallow hard, trying not to focus on the idea. But it doesn't make things any easier.

If these beasts don't leave, it's only a matter of time before other ones come to see what's up.

"Please!" I shout again. "If there's anyone out there! If anyone can help me… please come!"

Of course, no one responds. Honestly, I'd be kind of afraid to find out who would come here anyway.

I settle myself on the thickest branch, gathering my breath and thoughts… desperate to figure out what I should do next. I could jump down and try to make a run for it, but there's no way I can outrun these beasts again. I'm lucky I even managed to do it twice. Besides, I could run into something else. Something much worse. I could chance it and stay in this tree until the spiders get bored, but that's taking a huge gamble. I'm assuming they'll leave and nothing else will come.

And it does feel like something else will come.

This is the woods. Beyond the borders. Even the lairs, which seem safe, have been on high alert since Chocal tricked Arizona. And whatever happened to her, Taylis is probably assuming what happened to me. Maybe he thinks I wanted to offer myself to the *outsiders*. I've thought about it. I think I even said once or twice. But I never actually wanted to do it! It was just a passing thought. I don't want people to be cruel to me. I want to be with someone who likes me – loves me, even. Like my mom did. Even more so. And that's precisely how Taylis has been lately. But could it last? Even if I did somehow manage to make it back, will he believe my story?

I heard a female voice and chased it. Then giant spiders chased me. Here I am. LOVE ME!

Even in my head, it sounds stupid.

Taylis would never believe me. Even if he did, there's no way he could want me now. I ran from him once. Why shouldn't he think I would run from him again? I fought him about our relationship, and if I wasn't fighting him, he was fighting me. We never reached a point of clarity. Well, I didn't. Except for now, because staring down at those spider beasts and thinking about everything I had back at the lairs, there's only one thing I want more than anything.

And that's a future and family with Taylis.

Would he want me now? Even though I'm an alien? Even though I know so little about him? He's barely uncovered my past, but what if his is even more complicated? Will I ever get the chance to find out?

Well, it's unlikely if I stay in this tree all day.

It's almost staggering to think about a life with Taylis with so much certainty. I want him. I want to be Chosen mates. Officially. I want to start a family with him. I want to find the piece of happiness that Arizona found with Drozass. And if by some chance everything falls apart and we're separated, then I'm no worse than where I started. But at least I'll have memories to keep me going.

Down below, the spiders are still screeching, but no other animals come. Thank God. I don't think I'm ready to see what else this planet has to offer.

I stand on the branch, look down and try to figure out if there's any way for me to escape. To at least live. I don't want to die up here alone. I want to die trying to get back to the lairs so I can finally tell Taylis how I feel. So he can finally tell me how he feels. No drama. No questions. No miscommunication. I need one of those notes from middle school.

Check the 'yes' box if you like me. Check the 'no' box if you don't.

I'm stealing my nerves, preparing to jump down, when my worst fears come to life.

Another sound breaks through the woods. And it's making the spiders below freeze up and dart around. Almost as though they can sense something more dangerous than themselves is making their approach. I can't deny I'm getting pretty scared myself... especially when deep, masculine voices reach the translation device rooted in my ear.

"She's this way. I smell her."

"You sure?"

"Very sure. Two *fauders* are close to her. Sprogs. They'll run once they pick up our scent."

"Are there males nearby?"

"Not that I can tell. She's alone."

I curl my fingers more tightly around the branch, suddenly wishing I had run away minutes ago. At least then I would have had a head start from whatever is making these *fauders* scurry away.

Sidyths. I don't recognize their voices.

Arizona mentioned they don't sound like Taylis or the others.

The voices are deeper. Harsher.

Wilder.

I freeze, somehow convincing myself that if maybe they can't see me, perhaps they'll stomp by and I can make a break for home once again.

This planet really has turned me into an optimist.

ONCE THE *FAUDERS* FLEE THE SCENE, RELIEF SHOULD WASH OVER my body. But it's only replaced with a new fear — a different concern. The beings who approach are Sidyth, but they aren't the ones I'm familiar with. Their voices sound different in my ears, and though their language translates crystal clear, something seems off. Everything about them sounds rougher to me. I squint as the suns pour down, trying to locate a shape, and wondering if there's still time to run.

But I don't have it in me.

They know I'm there. Dread fills me when I realize they can probably smell precisely where I'm at.

Maybe I should be relieved that I can only hear two different voices and not a whole… uh… tribe, I guess?

And then another part of me is surprised I haven't heard a female voice. Isn't there someone with them? The whole reason I started this crazy journey through the woods?

But there's nothing else. Only two male voices chatting quietly amongst themselves as though they don't have a care in the world.

"She smells divine," one of them mutters, and I can hear his tongue slicking across his lips. "Can you smell that, Dyjav? A female! A real live female."

"She is still alien, Wybhir. Calm yourself. She may not even be pleasing visually."

"So long as she has a cunt, she'll be good enough for me."

I swallow hard. Of course. Why did I think these outsiders would want to sit down and have a conversation for a moment? Human males would die after a few months without sex. But aliens without it for a few years? I'm fucked in every sense of the word.

"Female?" one of them calls, though I can't see a face or shape yet. "Do you understand us, female?"

"Why are you speaking with her, Wybhir? What does it matter?"

"Perhaps she—" He stops himself short, not able to come up with a reason. That makes me shake with fear. These beings are going to take advantage of me. Steal pleasure without permission. I don't know why it fills me with such terror. Aliens have taken pleasure from me. I know how to handle it. Close my eyes and go someplace else, just like Arizona taught me. But things are different now. I know there's something better for me. If he even still wants me.

The voice comes again, shattering my thoughts of Taylis. "Female. We know you are here."

"Wybhir—"

"*Let me handle this, Dyjav,*" Wybhir hisses back. "Female, you should know there is no reason for you to try to run or become violent. Do you understand, female? Do you have a translation device?"

"Why are you even asking? What does it matter?"

"Quiet. Let the female speak."

I wet my lips. Should I say something? Is it better if they know I can talk or not? I'm not sure.

"Female," the one called Wybhir says in a soothing tone. "You cannot escape. We know you are up the tree — a smart move. The *fauders* cannot climb. You saved your life."

"Only to belong to us," the other – Dyjav chortles.

"Enough."

I shift amongst the branches, realizing they know exactly where I'm at, so there's no point in being quiet. It's broad daylight. Even if I could hide in the shadows, Sidyths probably know the woods better than I ever could. I'd only prolong the inevitable. I take in a deep, shaky sigh as the last of the trees part and two sizeable Sidyths stride right to the base of the tree where I'm 'hiding.'

"I see her," the shorter of the two says, pointing up immediately at my spot.

A prickle of fear runs up my spine. Looking down, they're staring back at me with eyes that remind me nothing of the Sidyths back at the lairs. Sure, they're gold, but that's where the similarities end.

They're both shades of blue, just like the Sidyths back home, but instead of scales, they're also covered in black ink which can only be described as tattoos. I don't want to think about how they got them. Or when. They couldn't have possibly had the tools to tattoo themselves while in double exile. Not only away from their home planet, but Prince Korben's cushiony set up. They're both incredibly fit looking with bulky arms, but instead of being shirt-less, they're both wearing white tops with no sleeves. The fabric is thin and tight, clinging to their toned abdomens, showing off what can only be eight packs. God. Maybe more.

If I wasn't so scared out of my fucking mind, I might even say they were ruggedly handsome.

But those differences aren't what catch my attention. It's the eyes. They're both staring up at me like I'm a two-hundred-dollar steak with lobster on the side and they've been fasting for a week. Like whoever devours it the fastest gets a second meal. And a third. And more.

I swallow hard and try glancing around, hoping that maybe there's a woman with them to at least give me a reason to think I sacrificed myself for something, but it's only the two.

The taller one – Dyjav seems to notice. "Looking for some-one, female?"

I shake my head, inwardly cursing as I make my fatal mistake. Now they know I understand them. Dyjav beams, showing off two pairs of very intimidating canines.

I try swallowing my fear, but since there's no point in hiding it any longer, I lean down. "Did you have someone else with you? A female, maybe?"

He chuckles. "No." He clears his throat and makes a weird screeching sound. The same one I ran to. When Dyjav notices my eyes widening, his beaming smile somehow grows wider. "I told Wybhir that my alien impression was good."

"I am impressed," the other – Wybhir admits, frowning before turning his chin up at me. "Are you coming to come down, female?"

"I can come up to get you," Dyjav offers, licking his lips.

"I suggest you come down on your own."

Instinct screams out at me not to give in so quickly, but years of being with Tanner have taught me well. I can either come down and not get punished for being difficult. Or fight. Be forcibly pulled own, disciplined, and get whatever they were going to do to me in the first place. I bite down hard on my lower lip as I clumsily make my way down the trunk of the tree, trying to avoid the hungry gazes of both Sidyths.

They look so much like Prince Korben and the others, but they're just not the same. Their bodies are leaner, more defined. Their eyes are crueler, and so much different Taylis'. God, I'd do anything to be back with him again. I don't care if he's grumpy. I don't care what kind of relationship he wants. I want to be with him. Deep down, I'd do anything not to have to face these two hungry Sidyths waiting below me.

They're going to take pleasure from me. That I can tell. The looks on their faces are enough to let me know it's inevitable. What they'll do next though, I'm not even sure. Maybe they'll rape me to death. Maybe they'll save me and keep me as their pleasure pet until I die. Maybe they'll share me with others. I guess whatever happens doesn't matter. There's nothing I can do to stop it — nothing I can do to get back to Taylis, Arizona and the others.

"So weird," Dyjav says, stepping around me as though appraising a pricey racehorse. "The skin. The eyes. The softness. How do they protect themselves?" He comes closer as though I don't have a voice of my own and pinches the flesh of my ass without hesitation. I yelp, resisting the urge to swat at him. "Touch her, Wybhir! See how different she feels."

I turn my gaze warily towards the second Sidyth, hoping he'll somehow help me out, but he merely draws closer, a stoic expression on his face. I don't move. My breath catches in my throat as his fierce golden eyes lower to my feet and then flick back to my hair. His hand lifts, and though I flinch slightly, he only hovers for a moment before seizing the end of my ponytail and pulling gently.

"Not there," Dyjav hisses, sounding bored. "The teets! The bottom. She is much softer there."

"I disagree," he says back, keeping his eyes on mine with my ponytail fully circled in his giant fist. "I like this thing. What do you call this, female?"

"Ponytail," I say quietly, not wanting Dyjav to hear for some reason.

"Yes." He yanks harder. "I like it. When I take you from behind, this will be most optimal. Do all females have these... poh-nee-tale?"

"If their hair is long enough," I say, hating that my voice is starting to tremble.

I hoped Wybhir would be the kinder of the two of them, but looking into his curious eyes now, I'm not sure. He's shorter than Dyjav, but that doesn't mean much when they're both hovering close to seven feet. And I can't ignore the look in his eyes while he pulls with my ponytail. *Take me from behind.* I wonder when he plans to do it? Within the next few moments? Does he have someplace he wants to take me first? A home? A settlement? Which Sidyth will take me first? Judging by the hunger in Wybhir's eyes, I have a feeling he's someone who likes to try things out before anyone else.

But despite that, there's a whisper of hope. Right now, they're only appraising me. Maybe someone's getting closer to help me. Perhaps Taylis is worried. Maybe he's tracking my scent. That's what Drozass did to find Arizona. At least... I think so? Damnit, I should have paid closer attention to the story.

While Wybhir keeps a tight grip on my long hair, Dyjav scouts the area around us. Looking upward, I realize clouds are settling overhead. Rain might be on its way.

"Female, do you have a name?" Wybhir purrs, pulling less-gently at my ponytail to capture my attention. "I am Wybhir. That is Dyjav." He frowns when I don't respond. "I expect that

Prince Korben has not spoken kindly about us to his stock. What did he tell you, female? That we are cruel? That we are wild?"

"Are you not?" I dare. "You are *outsiders*, aren't you?"

"I hate that term," Dyjav hisses, storming up to Wybhir's side. "Just because we didn't want to settle with him does not mean we are the *outsiders*. Maybe he is the *outsider*! He is the one who went against his father. The crown. The pride of the fatherland!"

"Enough, Dyjav," Wybhir grumbles. "You grow too passionate. If the female does not wish to speak, perhaps we shall. It doesn't seem fair that she's heard only one side of the story."

"I'll pass." I try to make myself sound bored though my nerves are making me shake like a chihuahua puppy. "I'm sure I don't need to know your background to endure whatever you two are going to do to me."

The two of them share a surprised expression. Dyjav is the first to speak. "I suppose the female is right," he says with a rough chuckle. "I told you, Wybhir. They are smart. So long as there is a cunt, though, that will be enough."

"*Is* there a cunt?"

"There are sprogs," he grumbles. "They have to stick their cocks somewhere."

"We have cunts," I say over the two of them, trying to convince myself that I'm buying time for Taylis to find me somehow. "All right? We have cunts for fucking."

"Can you carry sprogs?" Wybhir asks, his voice dripping with doubt.

"I could. But not now."

"Why not?" Dyjav hisses, looking impatient.

"I have a hormonal shot." When the two of them look at me strangely, I explain. "It's so alien clients don't have to worry about accidents. Pregnancy takes time. Time loses credits. Only if the hormonal shot is removed could a female get pregnant."

"Ahh." This answer seems to please Dyjav, and Wybhir thankfully releases my ponytail for the time being.

Why aren't they attacking me? They've talked about it since their approach, but now they almost seem more curious to learn about my anatomy than to use it. I should rejoice, but I still can't help but worry because it's only going to be a matter of time. And though Dyjav and Wybhir radiate cruelty, there's also a hint of curiosity there.

At least there is… until Dyjav removes his shorts and starts stroking his cock. "I will try her now," he declares proudly.

"Not yet," Wybhir hisses. "We need more information."

Just as I suspect, they do need something from me. And these males are so overconfident about their fucking abilities, they're probably worried about hurting me before getting the information they need.

Dyjav frowns, pulling his pants back up slowly with a pout. "We can ask afterward."

"What do you need to know?" I ask.

Wybhir whips around and grabs me by the ponytail so quickly I'm barely able to cry out as he bends my entire body backward, looming. "Patience, female. You will pleasure both of us. You do not need to be in such a rush. Though I'm sure you whores aren't used to having so much conversation."

I resist the snarl wanting to escape after hearing his condescending tone. But I need to keep it together. If they need me for information, and they're afraid pleasuring me will hurt me somehow, I can use that. I can buy time. If anyone is coming, I can buy some extra time.

"Now," Wybhir says, releasing my ponytail once more. "How many of you are there?"

"What do you mean?" I ask, feigning stupidity. It's my best chance of wasting time. Neither of these two thinks I'm smart anyway.

"You know what I mean. Females. We know Prince Korben has them. We want them. How many of them are there?"

"They have Chosen mates," I say airily.

"I care not," Dyjav hisses. "I want female cunt. Any female cunt. *Your* female cunt."

I suppress a shiver, but thankfully Wybhir doesn't seem on board with this. Not yet, anyway. "There are many of us here in other settlements. I don't know what Prince Korben told you, but we have been living off the land since he cast us away."

"Cast you away?" I croak.

"For not wanting to participate in his building of the lairs," Wybhir explains. "I wanted no part. There was no need. That's what he wanted. It was only a display to show who was loyal to him, and who was loyal to the cause."

"And who was loyal to neither, but made an example of," Dyjav tacks on.

"You don't believe in what Prince Korben believes?" I ask. "That females—"

"Females," Dyjav interrupts, "are for pleasure. That is it. I am not the only one who feels that way. But one female isn't enough. We need more to satisfy our brothers. We are willing to share, but we'll need more than you, female. I fear we'd kill you the first night."

I resist the urge to roll my eyes.

"Enough," Wybhir hisses, growing closer to me. "I want to know. How many females are at Prince Korben's lairs? A hand? Two?"

I don't answer.

A mistake on my part. I underestimated Wybhir's desperation.

His palm collides with my face in an instant, sending me flying backward.

CHAPTER 13

ALASKA

"I'm sorry," Wybhir purrs, pulling me back up to my feet. "Sometimes I lose my temper, yes? I'm not used to weak females being at the end of my strike. I had no plans to injure you truly."

"You're lying," I hiss, sniffing away the tears that threaten to fall. I don't want Wybhir to see them. Even Dyjav looks shocked by his actions.

"How many?" Wybhir asks again. "Please do not play with me, female. I'm not in the mood. I need to figure out how many of my brothers will have to share a female." He raises his hand, preparing to strike me again.

"Twenty!" I yelp. "There's twenty… uh… four hands."

"How many are mated?" he asks next.

"What does that matter?" Dyjav grumbles. "We're not on the fatherland. Those rules shouldn't apply—"

"How many are mated?" Wybhir asks over him.

"All of them." The lie comes too quickly, and as soon as it flies from my lips, I know they're never going to believe me.

Just as I feared, both Dyjav and Wybhir exchange glances, doubt written across their blue features. Hissing under his breath, Wybhir wraps his long, claw-tipped fingers around my throat without hesitation. I gasp out, but he doesn't squeeze. He doesn't lift. He holds me there. Nothing more than a reminder of who is in control here.

The predators and the prey.

"Tell the truth," he hisses in a low voice, crouching so he can look me straight in the eye. "We already know there are females. Surely our brothers wouldn't miss one if something, were to say, happen to her." Dyjav chuckles behind him "This can be easy or difficult, human. Tell the truth or—"

"I don't know how many are Chosen mates," I admit. And it's the truth. "There's twenty of us, but I don't know how many are officially mated."

"Lies," he hisses.

"I don't!" I yelp back at Wybhir. "I'm a loner. I don't spend a lot of time paying attention to others. You could… you could ask any of them. I keep to myself. Why do you think I came out here alone, and not with another Sidyth?"

They seem to consider this. Dyjav speaks. "You heard the other female. Were you looking for a companion?"

"No," I say, expression darkening. "I was just looking for an excuse."

"To get away from the others?" Wybhir guesses.

"Exactly. I wanted to get away. So, as you can see, there's no way I could know for sure how many are officially mated with Sidyths. But I do know some of them have sprogs."

Wybhir's eyes widen. "Young?"

"Who cares—" Dyjav interrupts.

"Families," I continue, hoping this is something important to

Wybhir. Surely, after everything that's happened to him, he wouldn't want to break up families. "Prince Korben has a daughter. So do some of the others. There are twins. There's another Sidyth. An older one. He lost his mate and sprog. He has a new mate now. He's trying to build a family again. They all are." I try to capture Wybhir's attention as he continues to mull this over. "You wouldn't want to take that away from anyone, would you? The happiness they've finally found?"

Wybhir frowns at me, almost as though unsure of what he wants to say. But just as soon as there is a flicker of empathy on his face, he blinks, and it's gone. "We all want that, female. Can't you understand? It isn't fair that some of our brothers are happy, and others are alone. You must understand. We want mates. We want females. If Prince Korben's connections brought him twenty alien females, surely he can find a way to order more." He pulls me close to him, hot breath pressing against my face. "Unless you'd like to be the mother for my brothers? We could share you."

"That could work as well," Dyjav agrees.

"There's no way Prince Korben could have more females brought in anyway," I say, hoping to keep them less focused on a gang bang. "I think he had to risk everything—"

"He could risk it again. We don't need twenty. Just enough to satisfy us."

I swallow hard, wondering if I dare to ask. "And… and how many are 'us'?"

Dyjav narrows his eyes, hissing loudly. "Don't answer her. If she returns to Prince Korben—"

"She's not going back to Prince Korben," Wybhir hisses back, shaking me bodily. "That is none of your concern, though. Why didn't Prince Korben tell you? Didn't he say how many were dropped off on the ship? Did he mention the originals?"

"Originals?"

Wybhir snorts. "Prince Korben *clearly* respects his stock of alien females. They know nothing. You know nothing. If you did, you would have never come out this far."

"Maybe not."

Still keeping me in his grasp, Wybhir shakes his head as though I'm a child too stupid or willfully ignorant to understand anything. And maybe he's not wrong for thinking so. If it's like he says, Prince Korben and the others didn't just keep one or two things from us, but an entire chest full of secrets. But why? Did he think we wouldn't be able to handle it? Did he think we would run away? The underground lairs... are they even necessary? Or was Prince Korben planning to keep alien females locked up down there if they didn't trust him and his brothers so easily?

Suddenly, I feel like I'm about to puke. But I have to fight anyway. No one deserves to be under the hand of Sidyths like these — not even Lacey.

"You can't bring in any other females," I start in a low voice, hoping not to upset Wybhir. "We humans... we didn't choose this fate."

"You are whores for hire," Dyjav sniffs.

"You think we chose that? We were tricked, forced to sign papers, and forced to spread our legs. If you bring in more females, there's no telling what the others will bring in. What if they take more people from my homeworld? Do you think anyone deserves that? Would you want someone to trick your loved ones into becoming space whores?"

An uneasy silence fills the air with my declaration, and for a moment, I think that they're considering what I have to say. Dyjav shifts uneasily, and Wybhir removes his grasp from the back of my neck, rising to his full height and taking a step backward. This is it. I've got them! They're listening! They're—

"I just want to fuck a cunt," Wybhir says. "I don't need to deal with this." He advances, and I hold up my hands, backing away with shuffling steps.

"J-just remember," I stammer. "If you kill me... your brothers won't have a cunt to fuck."

"Don't you kill her!" Dyjav grunts, elbowing his way next to Wybhir.

"I'm not going to kill her," he hisses back, reaching for my wrist. Somehow, I manage to escape him. "You heard her. Our brothers have mated with them. She will live. We will share this one with the others and—"

"But!" I yelp, searching for any distraction. *How does one distract a horny, seven-foot-tall alien?* And then I have an idea. "What if you're too big for me?"

He stops. Dyjav does too. My question caught them off guard. Wybhir pushes his tongue from his lips, probably tasting to see if I'm lying. But I guess he's happy with his find because he grips his cock in one hand as though testing the size. "Is this... is this possible?"

"Yes," I lie quickly. "One of the females was so small that when her mate tried to fuck her, *he killed her. Right on the spot!"* I put on the most horrific face I can imagine. "And when our females die? They emit a poison as punishment to the male for hurting her."

"You lie," Wybhir hisses. "This is not true."

"I saw it happen! Why do you think female humans are so inexpensive? Why Prince Korben could bring in twenty? It's because of the risk! He's already lost one of his kin. And it could happen to you."

"You said you had a pleasure mate," Dyjav remembers. "Your cunt can hold our cock."

"Can it?" I hold up my hands. "My pleasure mate will hate me if he ever finds out I said this... but he... he was tiny. So small that it did not hurt. I did not even know when he fucked me."

The horror that strikes both the male's faces would almost be comical if I weren't fighting to avoid being fucked by the two of them. "It would be a risk, you see. Because he was tiny. That is why we became pleasure mates. His dick was so small that it did not hurt me. But you both…" I drop my eyes down to their engorged cocks, hoping to build their egos while making them understand that fucking me could kill them, "… are much bigger than him. I fear you would be too much."

They're still thinking. As much as males want sex, I guess few males are willing to die for it. Or at least, these guys aren't. "You are saying," Dyjav begins slowly, "that human females have cunts than cannot be overfilled."

"Yes," I say, trying not to show relief.

"If the cock is too big… he could kill the female."

"Exactly."

"And the male…" Wybhir interjects.

"Human females release some toxin after death to the male who killed us. A male who does not recognize his girth is punished for taking a cunt too small for him."

"Your pleasure mate had a small cock?" Dyjav asks.

"*Minimal*," I add for effect. "I told you. It was hard to tell when he fucked me at all. Nothing like you. Even through your shorts, I can see that you are very well endowed, yes?"

Dyjav has the nerve to beam, lazily continuing his strokes. "I suppose that I am larger than many males. If your cunt is truly as small as you say, then perhaps I would be too much for you." His expression darkens. "Which is why we must bring in more. Then we can check if the cunt is large enough take me. Human cunts have accepted Sidyths here. Otherwise, there would be no sprogs. If I cannot take your cunt, I will take another's."

"What if she doesn't speak the truth?" Wybhir asks, going to reach for me again.

I jump back. "Why would I lie? You think I want to die?"

He hisses, knowing I have a point. "I do not pretend to understand the wishes of aliens. All I know is that delivery is coming soon. I want them to bring more of whatever you are. I will mention that we prefer ones with large cunts."

I resist the urge to grind my teeth. I'm running out of ways to waste time. And just because these two Sidyths aren't fucking me, doesn't mean others won't take their chances. Right now, I'm just waiting and hoping someone will come and help me out before Wybhir and Dyjav drag me further into the woods. There isn't much time left. Even this conversation has brought both of their cocks to full mast.

"Are you willing to risk it?" I try. "With the other females? How will you know your cocks will not kill them, therefore killing you?"

"I don't care any longer!" Dyjav shouts, growing frustrated and kicking at the dirt. "Prince Korben used his connections to get mates. It isn't fair! He should have ordered enough for all of us. We shouldn't have to live like this. Just because we didn't help build his underground dungeons doesn't mean we are bad. We want to fuck!"

"Calm yourself, Dyjav—"

"NO!" He roars, using his weight to push past Wybhir to come straight at me. He's got a crazed look in his eyes, and even Wybhir can't stop him now from pinning me up against the nearest tree. "It's been too long. If I am going to die, I am prepared to die today. So long as I can get my cock in your sweet, hot cunt. If I die, I'll die happily. And if I live? You shall be all mine." Without hesitation, he tears off my top, and I scream in surprises as my breasts spring free, and Dyjav buries his face in between them.

"The breasts..." Wybhir says, eyes full of wonder as he comes closer. "So soft..."

"Brother, you have no idea," Dyjav purrs, kissing my breasts roughly and sloppily tonguing my nipples. Humiliation washes over, but I don't struggle. *Struggling will only make things worse.* "Even if my cock will kill her and therefore kill me, I will die remembering this moment. These soft, wonderful teets. Do you see them, Wybhir? See how they move and bounce?" He pulls away, plumping them with both hands, fascination on his feral features. "It isn't fair that Prince Korben did not bring in more females! Does he think we're unworthy? Does he think we care that your cunts may kill us? Because I do not. I will die a happy male. Just like this."

"Let me touch them," Wybhir asks, drawing closer. "I want to touch them."

"Back off," Dyjav hisses. "Let me touch her. You don't know how much I've wanted this — longed for this even. When I heard Chocal talking about alien females with full, soft teets, I almost didn't believe him. But I feel them now. And now I only want more." His eyes meet mine. "Do your females ever have more than two of these? I should love to fill my hands with four! Maybe six. This is almost not enough for me." He's panting heavily now, barely keeping himself in control.

"I want to touch them," Wybhir says again.

"No. They are mine. This female is mine."

"We did not agree to that."

"Fuck the agreement," he hisses. "These are mine. These breasts are soft. They are meant for me. I don't need another female. I Choose this one."

"I'm taken," I try weakly.

"I care not. You are mine now, female."

"You could kill me if you try to pleasure me," I remind him.

"It would be worth it. Wybhir, move. I cannot wait. I want to claim her now."

"The female said—"

"Then, I will die first." There's no stopping Dyjav now. He's gone crazy. Even now he's shimmying out of his shorts, and his cock springs away from the fabric, pushing against my stomach. I gasp and squirm, but I can't bring myself to fight. There's no way I can overpower one Sidyth, let alone two.

But for the first time... I do care about an alien stealing pleasure.

I don't want it to happen.

I want to be back at the lairs. In my room. In bed. With Taylis. Grumpy face and all. Because he's my man. My alien mate. My Chosen.

"Please," I gasp, finding the words at last. "You don't want to do this. You'll die. I know you will."

"Dyjav, you should wait. Calm yourself."

"No! She is my female. I will do with her what I want." He buries his face into my hair, sniffing deeply. "She has been claimed by another. I suppose I can live with that. He has a small cock." He chuckles into my ears. "Besides, little female. I think you are lying. Not about your mate having a small cock, but about how a large one will kill you. I think you're lying to me to save yourself."

"I'm not," I gasp out, feeling his body shift as he drops rough kisses to my neck and collarbone.

"Tell me you're lying," Dyjav grunts, pressing around my folds. He doesn't entirely enter. Maybe he's afraid. Deep down, despite his sexual desperation, he doesn't want to die. "I need to hear it before I take you. Tell me it is safe to fuck you."

"You'll die." I can't tell him the truth. His head brushes against my core. I'm going to gasp out, and even though I don't want to, the sensation is too much.

"I won't. You're lying. It's safe to fuck human females."

"You'll die."

"Maybe you should believe her," Wybhir mutters.

"She's lying! I know she is!" He roars, still not quite able to push through.

"You're too big," I rasp. "I can tell. You're too big. I'll die. You'll die."

"YOU'RE LYING!" he roars at the top of his lungs.

"So do it," I scream back. "If you're so sure you won't die, just do it."

His face pulls away quickly. Those desperate, golden eyes sear right into mine. He's panting hard, and the scales on his neck are fully splayed away from his skin. He's going to call my bluff. It's only a matter of time. And then there will be nothing I can do. Dyjav takes in a deep breath, breathing hard.

"It can't be true," he manages between breaths, shaking his head. "But…"

"I think she's telling the truth, brother," Wybhir offers. "We should offer her to someone else. One of the punished. Then we can figure out what to do."

Dyjav's expression lifts just as mine falls. "That's not a bad idea, brother." Leaning down, he retrieves his pants and pulls them up to cover his dick once again. But I'm not relieved. "Why should I be the test? We have plenty of males who would be desperate."

"We wouldn't have to tell them how human females work."

My shoulders sag when the two of them each grab me by the arm.

"That's a brilliant idea," Dyjav says with a chuckle. "We should head back."

Then they're both pulling on me.

I'm moving further away from the only home I've known on Hethdiss.

And for once. I give a damn.

CHAPTER 14

TAYLIS

SHE WAS HERE.

The scent of Alaska fills the air in a clearing I've found, and she's not alone. She's still with two other males. Now, there's a trace of fear. A heavy scent of arousal, but it has nothing to do with Alaska. *These males have touched her and judging by the scent, Alaska did not enjoy it.*

I fight the urge to roar at the top of my lungs because I don't want whoever has her to know that I am following. Alaska is still alive. She may be damaged, but if she is alive, then that is all that matters.

I drop down to a crouch in the clearing where I scent the three bodies, trying to understand their movements by the patterns in the grass and earth. Horror strikes me as a flash of pure black catches my attention under the direct sunlight. Quickly, I scurry over the pile of black and scoop it up in my hand, the feel already achingly familiar. The strange alien texture presses against my fingers as I bring it up to my nose.

Alaska's top. They have removed it. Standing and darting around, I look for another pile of fabric, but thankfully, there is none. Which means they still may not have forced her to pleasure them. Which causes me to worry more. Why have they not hurt her? Why is there a scent of arousal, but no sign of pleasure? Are they saving her for something? Whatever the reason, it gives me a glimmer of hope, a reason to keep going under the beating suns.

I tuck the wisp of fabric in the band of my shorts, and keep going, making sure to pay close attention to the scent. Whoever has her is no longer bothering to cover her smell. That works for me but dread still bites because I don't quite understand what is happening to her.

She is alive. That is something I'll have to hold on to.

I continue at a fast pace, making sure to keep my steps light, so whoever has Alaska does not realize they are being followed. I want her kidnappers to be confident. I want them to let their guard down. It is only a matter of time that I may hear a voice. Confident males speak too loudly. Their steps become too clumsy. If there is any chance that they are moving less quickly than me, and I think that is a strong possibility because they have a female with them, I should be able to catch up.

But what am I going to find when I get there? I remember how haunted Drozass was. The desperation he felt to kill Chocal. Am I going to have the same desire? Will I be able to live with myself if I see Alaska's captors and don't rip out their throats right then and there?

I move more and more deeply into the woods, wondering if I should have started this trek alone. Right now, it would be nice to have one of the stronger fighters beside me. There are two males with Alaska and only one of me. Will I be able to fight them both?

In my haste to locate my female, I may not have considered my best options.

But there's no going back now. I've come this far. And I'm not going back to the lairs without Alaska in my arms.

And she will be my Chosen mate. Officially and forever.

And that's when I hear it. I stop in my tracks despite losing ground because I hear voices now. They are faint, but by keeping my steps quiet, I can almost distinct two voices ahead of me. But I don't hear a female. I don't hear my Alaska. Maybe they have not allowed her to speak. Maybe she is unconscious.

The idea makes me blaze with anger. Not only because of that, but because I cannot hear what the males are saying. I am close, but not close enough. I pick up the pace once more, hoping to catch a whisper of my mate's voice, but there is nothing.

Nothing.

She can't be hurt. She can't be hurt now! Not after I've come all this way!

Relief washes over. The voices hit my ears again, and this time I don't bother slowing down. I can't afford to. If they hear or scent me coming, then I'm as good as out in the open anyway. For only a moment, I wonder if I'm making a huge mistake. But scheita. It doesn't even matter now. I see faint shapes ahead of me – three distinct bodies talking loudly as though they don't have a care in the world.

Reckless. Fools. *These are the arslotas who captured my Alaska?*

It is almost shameful on my end, but I can't think about that now.

I'm close. I'm so close.

And then they stop. They turn slowly.

Before I have a chance to react, something substantial covers my entire mouth and pulls me away from their sight.

I try shouting out, but whosever holds me is much stronger than I am.

My hearts shatter because the voices start again.

And each step takes Alaska further away from me.

157

CHAPTER 15

ALASKA

"What was that?" Wybhir asks, glancing over his shoulder.

"What?" Dyjav follows his attention, his expression bored.

"Thought I heard someone."

"Probably those same *fauders* chasing the female earlier. You know those young ones don't give up on prey easily. The only reason they're not coming closer is because they can scent us around her"

Wybhir hums. "That makes sense, I suppose."

"Of course it makes sense," Dyjav chortles.

I can only hope the two of them are wrong and that someone, anyone has realized I'm gone and trying to find me. I want it to be Taylis, but whatever has been following us, is gone now and the woods have fallen silent.

"Besides," Dyjav continues, "this is our territory now. We're getting close. If anyone would be so stupid as to try and follow us out here would only have a death wish. Exten and Klose are out on guard tonight. If they scent anything, I'm sure we'll hear about it."

I swallow deeply. "Who… who are Exten and Klose?"

"No one you need to worry about, my Chosen," Dyjav says, stroking my arm tenderly. "They would be too rough with you."

"I'm not your Chosen," I hiss.

"You will be. I will make it so you will be all but begging me to keep you. Do not worry."

Another pit of worry forms at the base of my gut, and I fight the urge to puke again. "We're close," he said. Which means wherever these two are taking me… we don't have much further to go. And though Dyjav is saying I'm his mate, is he going to be able to stop other males from trying to claim me? Do I care either way? Maybe it's time for me to turn off my emotions completely.

But I can't now, not since Taylis.

He's awoken a fire inside me, and though so many memories are painful, the ones of him give me hope. Hope that he's not going to leave me to his wild brothers until I die.

"Not much further now," Dyjav says, smiling to himself. "We'll try you out with one of our more rebellious brothers to see how much you can take. And then, my Chosen, if you can take his cock and not kill him, I will take you next. And then I will fight for you."

"That's not part of the plan," Wybhir grumbles. "We need to get to the delivery. We need to get more females. That's what we need."

The arguing continues as the two of them lumber along with me in tow. Gods, I'm so afraid now. Once one of the other Sidyths has sex with me and not die, they'll probably try out another. And another. Before they realize they aren't going to die by fucking me. Which means that all human females are safe. They'll know I lied. And further, they'll know it'll be safe meeting the delivery and demanding they bring in more females.

"How are you going to do it?" I ask in a low voice.

"No talking," Wybhir hisses.

"Do what?" Dyjav asks at the same time.

"How are you going to convince the delivery guy to bring more females? You don't have any credits out here. As far as I know."

"What do you mean? We have a bargaining piece right here," Dyjav chuckles, jostling me slightly.

"You have no honor." I dare to curl up my nose.

"I do not need *honor*," Dyjav sneers back. "I've been cast from my home. They only made it seem like I believed in the cause. They needed more bodies because Prince Korben's father wanted to make it a production to have so many of us exiled."

"So you don't even believe in treating females with respect?"

"Of course not! Females are for pleasure and sprogs. That's all."

"Then why were you exiled?" I dare.

"Small crimes," he says in a low voice. "Many of us were."

"Like who?" I ask, suddenly desperate to hear the names. Is it any of the males who are with Prince Korben?

"Enough talking," Wybhir says, interrupting us both. "Whether Klose and Exten are close or not, it is not wise to speak so loudly in the woods."

"What about you?" I ask, turning my attention Wybhir. "Which one are you? Do you believe in the cause, or are you one of the small crimes males?"

"He's never told," Dyjav says, smirking. "I suppose it doesn't matter. He deserves a mate. We all deserve mates. And thanks to you, we'll be able to bargain with the delivery male to bring them in."

"So… you'll let him fuck me to deliver them," I reason.

"Exactly," Wybhir says.

"But how will you *pay* for the females? They cost plenty of credits – even if we are cheap to rich Sidyths. What kind of money will you use?"

"Don't worry about it," Wybhir says. "We have the payment."

I suppose that's that. Wybhir's jaw clenches, and I'm not foolish enough to keep pushing him. Thankfully, I don't have to. It seems that Dyjav is more than happy to fill in the silence.

"It's not a matter of having the credits, anyway, my Chosen. It's a matter of being able to give something to the male who makes the drop-off. You see, Prince Korben is aware that we are looking to reach out to him. But he wants to punish us for leaving his side. So unlike you, the rest of your females and his pampered brothers, we do not receive deliveries We live off what we can find on this planet. And let me tell you the food is not good."

"O-oh?" I ask cautiously, waiting for Wybhir to end the conversation. But he's only looking around.

"Yes. We're going to break through this time though. If we can get to the male who makes the drop, we can offer you to him. Then we can offer him payment to track down more females."

"How do you intend to… breakthrough?" I ask carefully.

Dyjav grins. "Some of the best males are with us. It should not be a problem."

"*That's enough*, Dyjav," Wybhir snarls, finally paying close attention to our conversation. "The cliffs are ahead. We are close. There is going to be quite the stir when we return with this pretty, soft-breasted female."

Cliffs? For some reason, I don't like the sound of that. And as much as I hate to admit it, I also see why Dyjav and Wybhir are upset. They're trapped on Hethdiss just like Prince Korben and the rest of the males. Shouldn't they be able to request food and supplies? Maybe not females, but other things? Doesn't seem fair that only those who stuck with him get to have luxuries. But I try not to dwell on it. It won't be much longer.

Males are going to steal pleasure from me again. Just like the old days. Just like before I came to Hethdiss.

I've taken so much for granted. Goodness. Kindness. All of it.

And now, it's going to be stripped away from me.

"Aww, do not tremble, my Chosen," Dyjav purrs after I realize I'm shaking. "Even when others take you, I will be there. Do not fret. You will be with me at the end of the day."

"Unless she is dead," Wybhir reminds him.

"Ahh, yes, I suppose that's true. Unless you are dead—" And then the two of them stop suddenly, and I almost spring free from their grasp, my bare breasts bouncing all over the place with their sloppy movements. I'm about to snap something, but Dyjav's tongue darts from his lips. "I heard it that time," he says in a lower voice.

"Yes. I fear that we are not alone."

"Where are Exten and Klose?"

"You think I know?" Wybhir grumbles. "I don't like this scent."

"What is it?"

"I smell... *her*," Wybhir says, lowering his chin down at me. "What is this?"

Me? But that can't be right... Taylis.

Hope explodes from my chest as the woods crash behind us and all around. Panicked, Wybhir and Dyjav both release me, practically flinging me behind their broad backs as the crashing comes closer and closer. Neither of the males has weapons, which used to be odd to me, but now it makes sense considering they're small-time criminals. I stumble back towards the nearest tree, preparing myself for anything, but in my heart, I know it's not a *fauder*. It's not a monster, but I'm sure it's a beast.

My beast.

"Taylis," I gasp when his large body breaks through the trees, and I see him clearly like something right out an action movie. *My personal Terminator.* And he's not alone. There are at least three other males with him and a female. Maybe two? *What the fuck?* Squinting, I almost can't believe the scene unfolding before my eyes, but it's just as I thought. It's Taylis. He came for me.

"Brothers, wait!" Wybhir shouts, holding up his hands. It gives them just enough time to hesitate, and Wybhir rushes back to me and grabs me by the neck. "You wouldn't want us to harm your little plaything, would you?"

It all happens so fast. Taylis drags his feet to a stop, staring right at me. "Alaska!" he gasps. "Did they hurt you?"

I try to answer, but Wybhir pinches my throat hard enough that I feel my breaths being cut off.

"STOP THAT!" Taylis roars, going to step forward, but one of his brothers holds him back. Drozass. "He'll kill her! He'll kill my mate!"

"Relax," Wybhir purrs. "No one wants to kill the female. She is quite valuable to all of us."

"She is my mate," Dyjav says proudly.

"No! She is mine!" Taylis shouts back, and out of the corner of my eye, I notice Dyjav's eyes widen.

"You? You are the pleasure mate with the small cock?"

If I were able to breathe, I might even be able to bite out a laugh at Taylis' horrified expression, but I can't even do that.

"Give her to me," he says instead, his expression darkening to something to deep and menacing that I've never seen him like that before. "Loosen your grip."

Wybhir does as he says, but only slightly. I cough loudly, not able to put my feet on the ground to steady myself. "If you go back now, we can avoid any lives lost. This female belongs to our clan now. She came to us."

"You tricked me!" I gasp out. "They can do this trick! This—" And just like that, Wybhir tightens his grip.

"The female is mine," Dyjav roars. "I will make sure she can handle my cock, and then I will claim her. Your small cock couldn't please her, but mine will… or I will die trying."

Several of the males blink, but no one says anything to his words. They're so ridiculous that I bet they don't matter much anyway.

But Taylis still looks angry, watching Wybhir hold me over empty air with hate in his usually grumpy eyes. The grip loosens again as there is a standoff between the two males and a mix of at least five males and humans. Wybhir and Dyjav have no chance. They're not close enough to their settlement. They probably know that. But the promise of sex makes any male desperate, I suppose.

"Give her to me," Taylis says with an eerie calm. "Now. She is a mated female. By trying to take her away from me, I am in every right to kill you. And you will die, *outsider*."

"Don't call me that!" Dyjav roars. "I don't care about your rules on the fatherland. Don't you get it? We are EXILED! None of this matters! Prince Korben does not matter! All that matters is living and dying and—"

"You will die if you do not give me my female now," Taylis finishes.

"There's too many of us," Drozass adds in. "You can't win. Give the female."

"No," Wybhir calls back. "She is ours. We are going to use her to bring in more females."

"What?" Drozass sounds shocked.

"You know this!" Dyjav shouts. "It is not fair for you to have females, and we do not. We are going to use this one and—"

"*Enough!*" Taylis roars, giving his brothers surrounding him a knowing look. Oh God. They're going to attack. And I'm right in the middle of it.

"Just put me down and end this!" I try, hoping that this won't have to end in blood. I have enough painful memories. I don't need anymore. "You can't fight them all."

"Even if we can't," Wybhir says, "there will be others. It isn't fair. We deserve mates too."

"You are filth," Taylis hisses.

"Stop that!" I dare to shout. Taylis' eyes widen. My outburst surprises me, but it's something I can't forget now. These males – these supposed *outsiders* – don't deserve to be punished more because they committed small crimes, do they? But then, I remember… they don't believe in treating female equally. *Females are for pleasure and sprogs.* I don't want another female to end up like that. It isn't right. It isn't…

"Let me go," I say in a low voice. "Let me go, and you may have a chance to live." I don't know if it's true, but I've got nothing else.

Just looking at Taylis' hardened expression, they're already dead.

"Fine," I croak, turning my attention towards Taylis. I realize now that he's been looking closely at me for this entire time. Almost as though waiting on a signal. *An okay to attack.* This close to Dyjav's and Wybhir's settlement, we probably don't have much time to lose. It's only a matter of time before others come, and I swear I hear rustling drawing near. I nod my head slightly at Taylis. *It's okay. I trust you'll keep me alive after all this.*

It's a whole lot of words in a small look, but Taylis gets the gist.

Like a spring in a mousetrap, with a slight nod from Taylis, the males lunge towards Dyjav and Wybhir, giving them no warning otherwise. I feel my body fly into the air as I'm tossed aside to save his skin. It all happens in slow motion.

Taylis going right after Dyjav and Wybhir running away. And

though I'm sure I'm imagining it, someone else is there watching the fight unfold.

I can't tell for sure, though. Because after that moment, the back of my head strikes something, and pain blasts through my eyes and red dots dance across my vision.

Then all goes black.

THE PAIN IS STILL THERE WHEN MY EYES OPEN, AND THE WORLD IS full of darkness. I don't know what time it is, where I am, or if I'm even alive. All I recognize is the pain. Flying through the skies and watching Taylis dart across the grass to murder the male who tried to claim me as his own. I open my eyes, and I notice the sky is somewhat familiar – blue and purple with two hot pink suns hanging overhead. It's not dark. It's still light out.

Maybe I'm not dead.

"Thank the Goddess!" a male voice calls out. "She's moving. Thank hell."

"Where did you learn how to use that word?" a female voice asks.

"Ellis taught me."

"Huh."

I'm struggling to understand what's happening around me, and the more I blink, the more familiar faces I see. Drozass. Hujun. The workout twins and Krista. I don't see Taylis, though. Oh, God, surely… surely…

"He's all right," Devyn says. "He went to take a piss. Had a feeling he didn't want to scare you while whipping out his supposedly 'small-cock.'" She giggles.

"Oh, man," Rene adds. "He's never gonna live that down. Did you tell them that?"

I'm struggling to focus, but everything becomes crystal clear when I notice movement out of the corner of my eye — a familiar shape. Large, blue, and though not overly bulky like Hujun, just as lithe and muscular as a Sidyth male should be. He's bruised, but otherwise… "Taylis. You're all right."

He steps towards me, dropping down to one knee. "I am. So are you. Thank the Goddess."

"I'm all right. Why wouldn't I be?" I bite down hard on my lower lip. "Did it look bad—"

"With what happened to Cade, I was so worried—"

I sit up straighter. "What happened to Cade? Is he all right?"

"He'll get there," he says, pulling me into his arms. "He'll get there, but for now you are what matters most. Your companion will tend to her mate. Allow me to tend to you." He squeezes me tightly enough that all retorts die in my throat. I can hardly remember what I was asking him about. Oh, yeah. Cade. I'll have to ask later. Because for now? All I can think about is the male holding me tightly. He's alive. I'm alive.

"What happened?" I ask in a low voice.

"The *arslota* threw you to try and save himself." Taylis' voice sounds more like a snarl. "But we got him. We got both of them."

"You… you killed them?"

"They had to die," Drozass adds in gently. "They kidnapped a Chosen female. Who knows what else they would have done if they got away with it. Perhaps this will send a message to those who think they can do what they please."

"Yes, but—" I stop myself short. There's nothing I can do about it now. I guess Drozass is right. They had to die. But it still seems a shame. If they conducted themselves better, if they believed females were equal, would it be such a crazy thing if more females were brought in? If this is indeed a utopia, wouldn't females who are whores end up happier here in the end?

It's almost too crazy to think about it. I don't want to. I want to focus on the male holding me tightly in his arms as though I'm his most prized possession. Maybe I am.

"Now that your female is awake, Taylis, we should start moving again. Get back to the lairs and inform Prince Korben about all of this," Drozass says. "I need to let my Arizona know that I am all right and… explain what happened to Cade."

I blink rapidly as Taylis swings me up into his arms, and our group breaks into a job. I realize now that the only ones here are Hujun, Drozass, Rene, and Devyn. But I saw two others.

"What happened to Cade?" I ask while Taylis continues to run.

"Don't worry about that now. Please. We will deal with it."

"I don't care that you'll deal with it," I grumble. "I want to know. Did someone get hurt because of me?"

Taylis doesn't answer. "Please. I just got you back. Can you please just shut up and let me hold you for a little while?" Still running, he holds me higher in his arms, nuzzling my hair with his nose. I have no idea how he isn't tripping over roots, and I can't bother to ask. He feels too good against me. It feels so good to be home. Once he pulls away, I notice his eyes are glassy.

"Are you…"

"I was injured," he says, but I know immediately that he's lying.

He's crying. For me. My grumpy, alien mate is crying because he's happy to have me back in his arms. And just seeing that, every wall I've ever built to protect myself shatters and crashes to the ground. I'm open. Exposed. Tears of my own spill without restraint, and I'm sobbing loudly into his shoulders. Taylis doesn't ask why. He knows why.

And that's why… he's my mate.

"Just tell me one thing," Taylis says, slowing his pace slightly once our surroundings become more familiar.

"Anything," I whisper.

"Tell me you didn't run from me this time."

I blink, and Taylis stops completely. "Is… is that what you think?"

"I know what I want to believe, but I want to hear it from you—"

"No," I say, wrapping my arms more tightly around his neck. "I heard a voice, and I just wanted to prove that…" I trail off, embarrassed by how silly it sounds now.

But Taylis' face is gravely seriously. "Prove what?"

"That humans aren't silly or stupid."

"What?" He's shocked. "My love, there may have been a time where I thought humans were fragile. Maybe even foolish. But the same could be said about anyone. I will tell you this now, though. You are not foolish. Nor fragile. You know this. You are my breathtaking, beautiful, strong, brave, and courageous female. And you are mine, yes?" His last sentence hitches so high with the question that the tears spill all over again.

I'm not sure if I'm digging this new emotional side of me, but I'll get used to it, I suppose.

With Taylis.

"All yours," I say, pulling him in for a deep kiss.

And damn… emotions or not… it feels so damn good.

I'm home at last.

EPILOGUE

TAYLIS

It **is glorious to have the female I have wanted in my arms as my Chosen mate.** For the past few turnings, I have done nothing but claim her. She is not ready to have her hormonal shots reversed, but that is something I will deal with in the future. For now, I am happy to claim her. Because beyond my bed, there is a heaviness in the air.

"The delivery drop will come in a few rotations," Prince Korben says in a low voice, shaking his head at the males surrounding him. There are human females in the Gathering Room at the central lair too, but that is only because we could not keep them away if we wanted to.

These females are part of us now. We are a family. A team. A clan.

We stick together.

"Just because Dyjav and Wybhir have been slain, does not mean there will not be others with the same desire," Prince

Korben continues, shaking his head. We have gone as long as we could hiding our females, but their curiosity along with our *outsider* brothers? I am afraid this issue is no longer avoidable."

Everyone in the room nods uneasily at one another. Hujun wraps his arm tightly around his tiny mate's shoulders and seeing him do so makes me want to do the same. There is a feeling of unease in the vast space, and every time a word is spoken, we cannot help but look over at Cade's mate – Dakota.

"When the delivery arrives, I want everyone there," Prince Korben says. "All males—"

"And females," Rene adds.

"No," Hujun rumbles.

"Yes," Devyn says, backing up her friend. "This is our clan, too. We want to help."

"What could you do?" Dash hisses. "What did you do to help Cade?"

"That is enough," Azan rumbles through his thick, red mask covering his mouth. "I say if the females want to help and they are not pregnant, they should be allowed that right. That is why we are here, yes? Why we are fighting?"

More nods.

"I'm so sorry," a small voice says beside me. My mate. "This is all my fault. What happened to Cade. What we're doing now—"

"Would have only happened eventually," I say in a gentle reminder.

"Agreed," Azan says. "This was a long time coming. We have sent a temporary message to those who think they can come and claim our females, but now we understand their true task. They want to reach out to the male who makes the drop. They want more females brought in."

"There's no way around it, I'm afraid," Prince Korben says solemnly. "I hoped this day would never come, but now that it is upon us, we must prepare. I am also hoping this will not end in bloodshed, but I fear it is inevitable. There is no fight without a struggle, I suppose. I wish…"

"What?" my mate asks.

"I wish we could speak to the *outsiders*. Maybe they can still be reasoned with."

"That's a death wish," Hujun rumbles. "They want females."

"That's not all they want!" Alaska pipes up. "I heard them. They want females, yes, but they also want the same things you guys have. They want food. They want supplies."

"Do you believe if we offered these things, they would leave us alone?" Prince Korben asks.

"Don't be foolish," Hujun grumbles.

"Some might be okay with that," Alaska says over him, shocking me to the point of making my cock bob in my shorts. My female is so strong. So brave. She has no idea. "It might be worth it to try. Even if only one is happy with this, that's one less problem, right?"

"And who would even dare to go on this mission?" Dash asks. "After what happened to Cade, can we trust these males to sit down and listen to what we have to say?"

"It can't hurt asking," Alaska says.

"What are you saying, female?" Dash snaps. "Will you go?"

Everyone falls silent, staring at my mate and myself. I want to fight for her. Demand that I'll never allow such a thing, but she speaks before I can begin.

"This all started with me, so I guess it makes sense for me to be the first to try."

"No," I hiss.

"Yes," she says back. "I want to do this."

"I'll go with her," Rene says. "I don't have a mate."

"Me too," Devyn says. "If Rene's going."

"We'll all go," Alaska says, turning up to look at me. "That's two unmated females and a mated one."

"I'll go too," I huff. "If I can't stop you from going."

"You can't."

I hiss under my breath, but Prince Korben speaks before I can start arguing once again. "It's a risk, but it may be worth it if what Alaska says is true. If food and supplies are what they want, we can certainly supply it."

"They want more than that," Hujun grumbles. "What they did to Ellis—"

"They will have males with them," Prince Korben speaks over him.

"When will they go?" Hujun asks next. "The drop is in a few days."

"Before then," Prince Korben says. "All unmated males—"

"I'm not going," Dash snarls. "I'll stay and keep watch on Cade."

"Very well," Prince Korben says, shaking his head. "If you change your mind—"

"I am not going to change my mind."

The group falls silent, all males glancing around at their mates; pleasure or Chosen. And though I am angry with Alaska for volunteering to go on this mission, I cannot also help but admire her. She spoke to the two males before they were slain. Perhaps she is right, and they only want food and supplies. Maybe there are only a few rebels who want females to keep them warm at night.

I cannot argue. Having Alaska by my side every night has been incredible.

And though I am worried about what must happen in the next few rotations, I am still newly mated to Alaska and have a particular urge that would help take the edge off. Rising to my feet, I pull my mate into my arms. She squeals in surprise despite the previous conversation. Dash sneers, but I try not to focus on that.

"Ahh," Dolan says, doing the same with his female. "Now that is a good idea, Taylis. Happy I wasn't the only one thinking that."

Some of the males and females remain, but most of those who have a mate, think I have come up with a good idea. There is nothing to be done now. Dash and Dakota are watching over Cade. The drop is not for a few days. The mission to the *outsider* clan will come, but not on this night. Which means there is something else to be done.

Something that would help clear my mind and the pressure building in my sack.

Once I have my female in our bed and on her back, I waste no time claiming her.

Trouble is coming. But for now, the only thing coming shall be my mate.

And myself... but only after my mate.

Mine.

Chapter 1
DAKOTA

Everything is different now. Though I shouldn't focus so much on the negative, I can't stop saying this repeatedly. I curl my hands into fists, trying to convince myself this is all a nightmare. That Alaska was never taken away by renegade Sidyths. That my pleasure mate Cade didn't stupidly volunteer to go on a hero's mission to help – only to get his dumbass hurt. *Fuck*, is it wrong to call my mate a dumbass? It doesn't seem okay since he's, well, yeah. Since he's not quite right anymore. Steeling my nerves for the umpteenth time, I rise from my spot in the Gathering Room and decide to check on him. Taya's sharp blue eyes glance over in my direction, probably wanting to say something, but what the hell can be said? I can practically hear her licking her lips as I depart, and I pick up the pace, not wanting to engage in any conversation with her.

I shouldn't care that Cade is hurt. We're technically not Chosen mates, and it's not like I was looking to have that sort of relationship with him anyway. Or at least, that's what I tell myself when the tears threaten to spill. Arizona wouldn't want me to cry. Alaska wouldn't either, but neither of them has any right to judge me when my man is hurt.

Ugh, Arizona, and her high standards. She was always preaching to us not to fall for an alien male client. Of course, she fell for a Sidyth first. Not that I blame her. As far as alien clients, these Sidyths are alright. Most are around seven feet tall, or even taller, and blue like the sexiest skinny leg pair of jeans I wore in high school. Scales like iridescent rainbows cover most of their bodies, and they're all built like professional football players. Oh, and most importantly? They don't force intimacy – not physically, anyway. Yeah, so I guess that's that. I understood why Arizona fell for one. She's older than most of us, even though she tries to hide it, and was probably getting the *baby itch* I always heard about. But Alaska? That's still baffling.

Or it was until I had more important things to worry about.

I turn a corner towards the back of the secondary lair on Hethdiss, sucking in a gasp when I hear stirring comes from Cade's private sanctuary. *Is someone in there with him?* He shouldn't have any visitors right now. Most of the secondary lair is preparing for yet another fool's mission about trying to reason with renegade Sidyths and making peace or whatever.

Peace. *Yeah right.* Friendship isn't going to turn my man into the man he used to be.

I swallow a sigh, hoping Cade won't hear me coming, because of course, he's alone in his lair. He must be awake. I wasn't always this afraid of seeing him. Even when nineteen other women and myself arrived on assignment, I warmed immediately to Cade. He was like most of the Sidyths in that he promised not to take pleasure without asking, but there was something else in his golden eyes. No, not a bug or anything like that. Three was a glimmer of humor. Playfulness. With the seriousness that comes with being an Intergalactic Call-Girl, I was shocked to see one of my clients smiling toothily in my direction. And Sidyths have a lot of teeth. Two large fangs on each side that could puncture a salmon's flesh better than a grizzly bear's claws.

I was kind of shocked he looked at me. Most clients look at Arizona first because she screams *sex*. Then they look at Alaska because she's all legs, blonde hair, and soft blue eyes Sometimes they even look at Kansas because to aliens, she's unique with a face covered in freckles. Usually, I'm the one hiding in the background with the State Girls, but no, this time, a client looked at me first.

I tried not to look surprised when his eyes danced across my frame. I'm supposed to be one of the top working Intergalactic Call-Girls, surrounded by the beauty that is Alaska, Arizona, and Kansas, but I must admit my heart skipped a beat the first time Cade looked at me. Others babbled around us, and there were some wails of fear, but I hardly noticed A seven-foot-tall, sexy alien man-beast was looking right at me, and not like he wanted to pin me down and fuck me ragged. Well, at least not without my permission.

It's not supposed to happen this way. Aliens are supposed to be our clients and nothing more. I should have made him work for my attention. That's how Arizona always told us how to do it, but it was hard for me because sometimes it felt like I was the one who had to work to get the attention of others. I couldn't talk to Arizona about it. She didn't understand, didn't care, or didn't have time to deal with my insecurities. She probably thinks I'm full of shit. I'm not ugly. I know that, sure. I have tan skin, blond hair, light brown eyes, and what some would call a 'bangin' body.' But compared to those who roll with me? I always felt like dirty Smeagol in the corner. I've never been able to hide my excitement when anyone (even an alien who paid for sex) selects me from a crowd.

How I ended up like this, I'll never know, but at least I can remember. *Because at least I have my memories.* I must remind myself of this always because something so simple as memory is something I can no longer take for granted.

Because Cade doesn't remember us first meeting. He doesn't remember how his eyes sizzled when they met mine, dropping down to my skirt and then back up to my eyes once again. He doesn't remember the first time he went down on me to see if I tasted as good as I smelled, and he sure as hell doesn't remember me returning the favor for the same reason. No, Cade doesn't remember any of that because he doesn't remember me.

After Alaska realized she had feelings for a Sidyth, as usual, she did everything to hide it. In Alaska terms, that means being stupid and making stupid decisions. I don't know how someone can be so dumb as to not only runaway once from this safe little setup, but twice. But that's precisely what Alaska did to prove she didn't have feelings for Taylis – her pain in the ass Chosen mate. Don't get me wrong. I would be happy for her. *I would*, if not for her stupid runaway bride issues because that's what caused troubles in the first place.

One night, I guess she heard voices or whatever beyond the safety barriers on Hethdiss set up by Prince Korben, Hujun, and a few others, and decided to check it out. The females are already supposed to be on high alert after Arizona was nearly stolen away by a Sidyth named Chocal in exchange for earning good graces with *outsiders*, or something, but Alaska didn't care. She heard voices. She went after them. And she got caught by two Sidyths who aren't exactly on the same page as the ones we're living with. No. These Sidyths don't want to treat women fairly, or even nicely. When they want pleasure, they take it. They also don't believe in Chosen mates – not anymore, anyway. They wanted to share Alaska with their brothers at some other unknown settlement on Hethdiss. And that would have happened, if not for Taylis and his merry band of following heroes.

Which included my Cade.

He always wanted to play the part of a hero. He's always looking for trouble. He's continually trying to prove how badass he is by getting into fights with his brothers. He calls it sparring. I call it a big waste of time and energy. But it was cute in a way because looking back on it now, at least I didn't have to worry about him ever getting hurt. I should have known something terrible would happen to him when he left the lairs to help out Taylis. My man is tough, but my man's mentality is *action first, think later,* so of course, the worst possible thing happened to him.

Dash told me he ran in, and I guess one of the other Sidyths somehow grabbed him or threw him, or something. I don't know exactly, and I don't think Dash does either. The important part is that Cade hit his head somehow, and now his mind is blank.

Not completely. Just most of his recent memories have vanished.

He remembers his mother, father, and extended family back on his homeworld, Sidetha. He remembers his exile. He even remembers hearing Prince Korben's plans to bring in human females so his brothers could have mates. But everything after that is a blur.

And a few long days after his injury, it still is. I should be grateful. Cade's not dead. He's not unconscious, and Chentan was able to work some alien medical magic to get him up and talking again. It's all good except that while he's technically like himself, he's nothing like himself at all.

Arizona and Alaska tell me repeatedly I should be happy he's alive. He has some memories, so there's a good chance he'll get the rest back. Maybe he'll even remember the promises he made to me. Maybe this and maybe that. *I'm tired of hearing, maybe.* I'm tired of being happy that he's alive when I want so much more. It's only been a few days, and we have so many more important things to think about with *outsider* Sidyths growing dangerously curious about the human females. *Yes, I know all these things!* I still want my man back. I want him to remember me.

"You've got to keep it together, girl," Arizona said the night everyone returned before I could see Cade. She shook her head as though she had something to be upset about. "Just because he doesn't remember you now, doesn't mean he won't remember you later. These guys are strong, you know. Look at my Drozass."

I fought the urge to snarl. *If Drozass is so strong, why didn't he stop my man from getting hurt?*

And Alaska. I didn't even want to look at Alaska when she returned. She kept saying sorry, and she looked less like a robot than usual, but what the fuck did that matter now? How could it mean anything when she's safe with her Chosen mate, and mine's hurt because of them?

I managed to silence my complaints, remembering that at least Cade would have a chance to gain his memories back, but at the time, I wasn't only devastated, I was angry. Fucking livid.

I didn't think this would happen. He said he loved me.

It sounded so cheesy after something so terrible just happened I couldn't get the words out without my voice cracking. No one knew Cade had Chosen me to be his mate. We never had a chance to tell Prince Korben. And now being hurt, I don't feel like I have any right to claim him.

What if he doesn't recover? I'm not prepared to be a twenty-two-year-old widow.

"Hey, relax. Don't act like he's already dead." Kansas sounded incredibly awkward for some reason that first night, and though she's usually not that pleasant to begin with, it almost felt like she wanted to leave the conversation entirely. I'm still not entirely sure what's up with her "They said it was a head injury, right?"

"Right," I muttered. "I don't know… I mean, Chentan doesn't know how much he remembers yet." I pressed my face into my hands, trying to hide my emotions. Usually, Arizona didn't like it, and though she's changed since mating with Drozass, old habits die hard, I guess. "What if he's really hurt? What if it's more than his head?"

"He's going to be fine," Kansas insisted, looking shockingly concerned. "He has to be fine. He must be. If anything, Dash will throw a fit if—"

"I don't give two shits about Dash right now." Kansas looked surprised by my words, but I didn't give a damn. *How could she talk about her man while mine was hurt?*

But I knew they were only trying to help.

The first night he awoke, I tried talking to him after I found out what happened. Chentan tried being patient, but I refused to believe his diagnosis at first.

Cade lost his memory. He doesn't remember me? Doesn't remember us? Shit happens like this in real life?

I ran into Cade's room and went to wrap my arms around him, but he slapped me away, called me 'female' and demanded Chetan to explain. After some begging, I finally convinced Chentan to leave me alone with him. And after some more begging, I convinced Cade to let me stay and talk to him directly.

That night, I did everything to jog his memory. I even tried touching him, waiting for that flicker in his eyes to appear once again — that same sizzle when we met eyes for the first time. I told him about the times we spent together and how he wanted us to become more than pleasure mates. He sat in bed and listened so patiently, so unlike the crazy, wild, bursting bottle of energy I'm used to dealing with, and that should have let me know that something wasn't right. I tried not to take it personally, but it was hard when just hours ago he was telling me he loved me and wanted to speak to Prince Korben about becoming Chosen mates.

When I finished telling Cade all I could, he merely kept sitting there. Staring. Silent. Blinking.

And when he spoke, his words hurt more than anything I'd ever heard before and probably will ever hear again.

"You tell lies, female. There is no way I would love an alien — especially one as primitive as a human."

I didn't think his words would hurt so much. I've been dealt some nasty cards as the least memorable member of Arizona's crew, but I always managed to brush it off. But seeing Cade in bed, his eyes still puffy, but so chilly and detached, I felt my heart breaking. It shouldn't matter that he feels this way about me. For all I know, this assignment could end, and Cade and I would be separated. It's not like we have a family, and no one knows we planned to be official mates. If anything, I should have felt some relief – if I was a cold-ass bitch like Alaska. But I'm not, and his words stung me so harshly that I had to take a seat, clutching at my chest to keep my breathing steady.

"Are you ill, female?" Cade asked, sitting up straighter in bed, but making no move towards me. "You should leave—"

"You don't remember?" I gasped, lifting my chin as tears began to spill. "You're not joking around? You don't remember me?"

His eyes narrowed. "No."

"You don't remember us?"

"There is no us, female."

The tears welled up without permission. He never looked at me this way. Not in the entire time we've known each other. He looked at me as though I was a stranger – any annoying one, at that. "You said you loved me. You said you wanted us to become Chosen mates."

He hissed. "Impossible."

Pinching my eyes shut, I still remember the sting in his words that first night. He's gotten softer with me, I think a few days' worth of memories have trickled back to him, so at least he remembers my face, but that's about it. I don't really know what else I can do now but hope to hell that Arizona and Alaska are right, and his memories will slowly return.

They must come back. I don't want anyone else here, and there's no way I'm leaving Alaska, Arizona, and Kansas. Hethdiss is my home now. My mate is Cade. How can I possibly turn off a year and a half of a relationship with the sexiest, cockiest piece of man meat that ever barged his way into my life, and my legs for that matter? Sometimes I wish we both lost our memories. Maybe things would hurt less that way. But that's not an option. And even if it were, I would never take it.

I must find a way to bring Cade's memories back.

He loved me once. I'm sure I can find a way for him to love me again.

Some of the males here think I'm a fool to spend time with a male who can't even remember me. He's not the same as he was. Whatever special connection we had is now severed, and if Cade didn't immediately feel something for me after waking up, he's probably not going to feel it again. Chentan tries being patient, but part of me wonders if he's only so kind to me because he's unmated and now has a shot for a human female of his own. But I don't want just any Sidyth. I want Cade – the first man who looked at me before any of my friends. The first alien who made me feel I have more to offer than a tight body and a decent face. He was my love. My everything. And now he can't even remember who I am.

I should have known it was too good to be true. After all, what person expects to find love after becoming an Intergalactic Call-Girl? Julia Roberts found happiness, but she wasn't boning aliens, and neither was the chick in that geisha movie where she ends up with a customer. Aliens don't think humans are worth a damn, at least not any of the ones I've worked with. I didn't know I would find anyone to love, let alone anyone to love me. Notably not some cocky, smirking blue alien like Cade. But he drew me in with those eyes. He made me feel like I had so much to offer. He didn't look at Taya and her tiny frame, or Drey's incredibly sexy face with a permanent 'smize in the eyes.' He wasn't even interested in Mia's model frame and somehow adorable sneer. He scanned the crowd and found my eyes and didn't look away. And that Cade – that same Cade – only calls me 'female' and snorts every time I try to explain to him that we're mates.

It hurt so much that because of Alaska's happiness, I had to become miserable. If she hadn't been so set on proving to the world that she felt nothing for Taylis, my man would be safe. If she hadn't run away, Cade would still be with me. Prince Korben wouldn't be worried about renegade Sidyths and sending some of my friends away to make sure no one else tries to steal human females. I'm not saying I wanted to stay on Hethdiss forever. Or maybe I am. I don't even know anymore. Sometimes my memories feel as hazy as they must for Cade. Expect my loss is by choice. I must remember that Cade isn't doing this to be funny, and he isn't doing this to piss me off. And for some reason, that hurts even more.

Cade's been my partner since I arrived on Hethdiss. I've never been with as kind an alien as him. Most people think he's just some cocky, overbearing asshole. But that's not my Cade. That's Dash – Kansas' mate – but I'm not about to get into that story. The point is, Cade in public isn't the same male as he is in private. He's gentle. He's caring. And funny. Goddamn hilarious. He made me laugh when I didn't think I would ever be able to smile again.

No one else understood our relationship, and I was perfectly fine with that. I didn't want anyone else to see Cade the way I did. I wanted that part of him to be just for me. I didn't want anyone else to know that he liked to tickle me in bed to hear me laugh. I didn't want anyone to see that he kissed me on the forehead because I told him how much I loved seeing it in the movies. I wanted all those soft, vulnerable parts of Cade to belong to me, and I didn't think it was possible to find someone like that while working as an Intergalactic Call-Girl to fill that role. And I had it.

Damnit, I had it all until Alaska fucked up and ruined everything, which left her happy and mated, and me lost and miserable.

Now, I'm just waiting. Every day is a waiting game. Every day is about schedule and routine. An agenda I'm no longer used to. Every day I visit Cade and try to help him remember what he lost. I wait with bated breath, hoping one story will force him to blink, and everything will come rushing back. That he'll look at me the same way he used to look at me.

That he'll say he loved me as he said to me before my entire world on Hethdiss shattered at my feet.

Fuck, and now I'm getting emotional again. Cade won't want to see me like this. I sniff loudly, hating that it will draw his attention to the lair opening, but I don't care. I can't cry. I've cried more in the past few days than I've cried my entire life, and Cade doesn't give a shit about any of it. I'm just the female who comes to his room, nurses him and feeds him lies. Talk about a thankless job. But I wouldn't do it any other way. Chentan says speaking about the past may help him remember if that's something I want to happen. Of course, I want it to happen!

I push the curtain aside.

Cade's golden eyes widen when they settle on my face, and for a moment, I hesitate. He's quiet. *Is he… is it possible… does he finally remember—*

"You again," he says in a low voice. "You really can't seem to get enough of me, can you?"

I resist the urge to sneer at him. Usually, a comment like this would be said in a flirtatious manner, but Cade's frown lets me know he's earnest. I try not to let that bother me. I put on my best smile and treat him like he was any other client. *A client who I happen to be in love with.* "You're as charming as ever, Cade. How are you feeling today?"

He rubs his forehead with two blunt, blue fingers, fixing his eyes on mine once again. Almost as though he's trying to coax out some hidden memory. I frown, hoping he's not in pain, as he sits up higher in his bed. Our bed. "I feel fine. It is Chentan who wishes for me to stay in this bed and endure these conversations. It is part of my treatment."

Treatment. Well damn.

This is going to be another hard day with the man I love.

CHAPTER 2

CADE

"Don't hurt yourself, Cade. If you keep rubbing at your forehead like that, you're going to give yourself a headache."

I can't help but shoot a frown in the alien female's direction. Dakota, she says her name is. How strange. Feels funny against my forked tongue, but I don't dare mention this on the off chance that what she's been telling me turns out to be correct.

I am mated to an alien. I don't want to believe it even if Dakota is one of the tastiest looking beings I've seen in a long time.

"Do not worry about what happens to me, female." I can't help but sneer, sitting up straight in bed and shoving the blanket aside, so the sun rayers perched around the corners of my lair hit my skin directly. Chentan will not allow me to leave the lair, so I'm already weak and depressed. Now I must deal with this same human visiting me once again and having the audacity to be concerned. "You should be more concerned about your health. Humans are fragile and weak. I'm surprised you managed to walk here without tripping over your tiny feet."

She rolls her eyes at me. They are an odd color. Like mud… under a dying sun. "I'm just saying to be careful. You don't have all your memories back—"

"So you say," I hiss.

"So *everyone* says," she hisses back. "Chentan, Prince Korben, Dash, Hujun, Azan, etc. How many more people need to tell you that you've lost your recent memories? Why would anyone lie about that?"

"Perhaps to trick me into taking a human female as a mate."

She sucks in a breath but doesn't retort, leaning against the nearest wall and crossing her arms under her tiny, but soft-looking breasts. It's hard not to look at the female even though she is a human, and therefore an alien to me. I don't want to believe I have taken a mate and somehow forgotten about it, but Dakota is not the only one saying this. The others say the same things. Dash would not lie. Drozass would not, either. But how? How could I forget something so crucial as Choosing a mate? The thought makes me incredibly angry, and I hiss sharply under my breath.

"That's enough of that," Dakota says. "It's hard to accept, but that's how it is, Cade. If you don't want to believe me, fine. But I know you believe your brothers."

"You don't know what or who I believe."

She rolls her eyes, shaking her head as though ashamed by my behavior. And though I would never tell her so, I must admit that she deals with me with the same finesse my closest brothers do – as though she knows me. It's frustrating and frightening at the same time. I've heard the stories many times, not only from Dakota but my brothers. This female is my pleasure mate and has been since the arrival of the humans to Hethdiss during our exile. Dakota adds another piece to the story – saying that I planned to Choose her, but none of my brothers can confirm this. And though I want to call Dakota a liar and send her away, something softly stirs in the back of my mind, warning this would be a huge mistake.

Every day I try to focus on what I do remember. I was exiled from Sidetha. I arrived on Hethdiss with some of my closest brothers. There was a *divide* when we landed and many struggled as we built the underground lairs. Prince Korben never specifically said why they were necessary at the time, but I listened to his orders because I wasn't sure what else to do. I was not prepared to be an *outsider*, and for the most part, I agreed that females and males should be treated fairly and equally. I remember the time passing, and I even have faint memories of pictures Prince Korben showed to all of us – files and photos of twenty females. But not Sidyth females. No. They were aliens. Humans. Small and curvy. Pale and with a variety of colors and textures upon their heads. I remember how disappointed I was to find out that we could not afford something less primitive.

I had no interest in Choosing a human female as my mate.

But now I have been thrust into a world where others say different.

It's not that I believe that my brothers are lying to me, but I cannot imagine looking at the human female standing before me and deciding that I must have her. She is beautiful, yes. But she is still alien. And though she causes a stirring in my cock, I am sure that must be because of the loneliness. I haven't experienced any pleasure, but no matter how hard I try to convince others of this, they promise this is not the case. They say Dakota is my female. My pleasure mate. We have had sex. *How could I have sex and not remember? Is my mind so weak?*

When I learned how I lost my memories in the first place, I did not want to believe it, either. Nothing added up. Me? Help Taylis bring back his stolen human? Fight my brothers (even if they were *outsiders*)? Having them fight me back to the point of throwing or knocking me against a tree? All of this for some female I don't care about or even know? It's not that I don't think I would do it, but it doesn't make sense compared to what I know. And the worst thing of all is that I'm not even sure if I can trust what I think about I know about myself when Dakota stands across the room from me, insisting that I Chose her as a mate.

Chentan tried to get me to believe everything was true except the part about Choosing Dakota as a mate, but I wasn't having any of it. I don't feel like I've lost anything. My brothers keep saying a massive chunk of my memories is missing because of what happened with the *outsiders*, but how can I believe anyone when I don't feel like anything's wrong? I don't like the idea of them being right because that means I'm wrong, and so I keep fighting and fighting against the idea entirely.

"How are you feeling today?" Dakota's voice dances across the lair and straight to the tip of my cock, which drives me insane. I quickly pull the sheets over my waist, so she doesn't see my physical reaction to her. She's going to think something is wrong with me. And apparently, something very much is.

"I told you to worry about yourself, female," I say, trying to make it seem as though I am too busy for her company. The human isn't having any of it, coming up to the bed and tucking the sheets more tightly around my waist. "What are you doing?"

"Fixing your sheets."

"I am not a sprog," I grumble, wrenching the sheets away from her tiny, pale hands. "I do not need *you* to take care of me," I swear, if she gets any closer, I'm going to have to stroke my cock when she leaves, and something seems so incredibly wrong about that. She is an alien. A human. A primitive female. Surely, I'm better than this.

"You think I don't know that? I'm only trying to do the right thing since you're supposed to be my—" She stops short when I lift my chin and flash a look of annoyance at her. I know what she's going to say, and the last thing I want is to hear it. Her shoulders tremble, and thankfully, she removes her hands. "You still don't remember."

"No. I do not."

"Maybe you don't want to."

Lies, my mind immediately shouts inside of my head. *Does she think that I like being the way I am?* Can she possibly believe I like hearing that a large portion of my life has been wiped from my memory, and I don't know it? I hate this. I hate looking at this beautiful human female and having no idea who she is. My life was comfortable – even in exile – I had my brothers, so I had no reason to think about finding a mate, seeking pleasure, or building a family. And because of that, I would have been fine knowing I was still alone on Hethdiss.

But this female had to come along and ruin everything with her curvy body, short yellow hair and intense brown eyes.

I bite back a sigh. "I am sorry. But that is not true. I do want to remember things, but you must understand. I don't feel as though I have lost anything."

"So, you feel fine?"

"I feel… fine," I grit out, fighting my excitement as the female sits on the bed and takes my face in her fragile hands. I try to look away.

"So, when you look at me. You feel nothing. Nothing at all?"

I bite down hard on the inside of my cheek, swallowing my arousal. There's no way she can't feel my cock brushing up against the soft curve of her bottom. Dakota tells me this is some- thing I liked when we were mated. I wanted her perched in my lap, and she liked feeling small against me. She tells me no one understands our relationship because I come across as such an *asshole* when I love making her feel, tiny, soft, and protected. We've apparently had many conversations late into the nights about our futures, our wants, needs, and desires. We've spoken about her home on Earth, and mine on Sidetha. She tells me so many things. She knows things about me that I don't think I would have told anyone unless I planned to Choose them, but I cannot remember. And I hate not remembering. I hate not recognizing *her.*

"I'm sorry," I manage to grit, hating how my voice sounds so strained.

And even more, I hate how desperate I am to pull the female to me when the look of genuine disappointment flickers across her soft features, and she climbs off my lap and returns to her spot across from the bed.

Chentan says I need to look – really look – at Dakota and search my mind for any tidbit of memories about her and everything could come flooding back. I should be doing it, but I'm afraid that when it happens, I'm going to find out that Dakota wasn't lying. And if she wasn't lying, then it's as she said. I'm her mate. And therefore, I'm a weak male with a weak mind because I couldn't hold on to the memories of us just because of a simple head injury. No matter how great it would be to have those memories back, and remember this female again, it would still be painful to remember these past few days, when I didn't know anything about her when I called her a liar. Even if I do get my memories back, could Dakota even want a male so weak?

"It's… it's alright," Dakota says from across the lair, pushing a hand through her hair. "I shouldn't have done that. It was inappropriate."

"Even though you say I'm your mate?"

"You say you can't remember."

"Ahh, but you say you can," I find myself saying, shocked by my own words. "Were you trying to help me remember? You once said to me that I liked when you sat in my lap, yes?"

Her eyes flick up to mine. "Yeah. I like feeling small."

"And safe," I mutter. "I know you may not believe me, Duh-co-tuh, but there is nothing I want more than to remember saying these words."

"Saying them to me? Or just saying them in general?"

I try not to scowl. "Saying them to you."

She sniffs unattractively, lowering her head and swiping a hand across her face. "Goddammit," she says in a thick tone. "I promised I wouldn't cry in front of you today. I know how much you hate it."

Something stirs in my hearts. "I don't hate it." I hate the tightening feeling in my chest when the human tears up. "It's just hard for me to see. I don't understand. I don't want to see you upset."

"I know, I know," she mutters, swiping harder at her eyes. "I just… crying isn't going to help anything."

"It is not. But please do not think I *hate* you crying. It is not you I hate. It is me for being unsure of what to believe."

She sniffs once more, finally lowering her hand completely. "R-right. Cade, do you mind if I ask you a question?"

"You are in my lair and supposedly my pleasure mate. You can ask me anything."

She frowns but quickly shakes it away. "I'm starting to think it may be a bad idea to keep coming here." My face falls, but luckily Dakota isn't paying enough attention. "I know it's only been a few days, but I don't think things are getting any better, and maybe it would be easier if we just…"

"Just… what?" I hiss, my expression darkening. I don't like this. Yes, the human female is confusing, but this does not mean I don't enjoy her company.

"Maybe we should just stop talking to each other so much—"

"No." The words fly from my lips before I have the chance to stop them. But I don't regret them, even when Dakota's eyes lift, and her expression is a look of pure shock. I clear my throat. "No. Chentan says I have lost memories, and you are a big part of them. If this is all true, then keep coming here. Keep talking to me. Keep attempting to jar my memory. I want my memories back. I don't like feeling as though I am inferior."

"Feeling inferior. Is that all that concerns you?"

I hiss. "You know it is not."

She takes in a deep, shaky sigh, and I can't help wondering if I've played this all wrong. A female would not act like this if she were pretending to be my mate. No female is that cunning. Dakota speaks the truth. Me and her, no matter how crazy it sounds now, shared something, and now it has been stripped from her and stripped from my memories. No matter how much I want to fight it, my life is connected to this female, and I'll stop at nothing to understand what we had.

"Alright, then. I guess I'll keep stopping by. But you know? You don't have to be such an ass all the time. My name is Dakota, not female." Her lower lip juts out, and it's such an erotic sight that I nearly groan, fighting off the images of sucking it between my lips.

"I called you Duh-co-tuh earlier," I remind her.

"Dakota," she says in that quick, articulate tongue.

"Dakota," I mimic perfectly. "There. Are you satisfied?"

A flicker of a smile crosses her features. "Things could be worse, I suppose," she says, crossing her arms back across her chest, pushing up those fluffy tit pillows once again. For some reason, I know they're soft and not just because they look that way. It's odd…

"I could have no memories of anything," I say.

"Or, you could be dead."

I can't help chuckling. "It's going to take a lot more than an *outsider* to kill me, female. Do not worry. You are stuck with me, and I am going to get my memories back."

"Who says I'm worried?"

"I do."

The verbal play almost feels familiar, as well. It's odd to get into these playful conversations with the alien female because they cause a tickling and stirring in the back of my brain. Something lurks there and knowing that, I feel myself growing frustrated and annoyed. I don't want hints and whispers of my past and memories with this female. I want them back completely. And I want them back now. I stare hard at the female leaning against the wall, trying to decide how desperately I want to remember her.

Scheita. There is nothing I won't do.

"Cade," she says clearly, catching her attention. "Chentan mentioned that spending more time with you and touching you may bring back some of my earlier memories."

"Yeah?"

"Well, I'm wondering if maybe that's not such a bad idea." She comes closer to the bed and gently eases the sheets away from my waist, exposing my engorged cock straining beneath my shorts. Dakota doesn't look the least bit surprised. "Your body has memories of me, even if your brain does not. Maybe we should keep pushing this. Try to force some of your memories to come back."

"Force them? How did you think we could do that?"

She slicks that short, pale pink tongue across her lips, and my cock violently bobs at the sight. My reaction to this alien isn't normal. I can't ignore that. "Like when I straddled you," she reminds me.

"You believe more physical interaction could stir up my memories." She nods as I consider her offer. "That is an interesting suggestion. I don't know what's happening with me, but I know my body has a powerful reaction to you. And if my brain wants to be difficult, then maybe we should try more aggressive tactics. It makes sense."

"It does?" She sounds surprised at first but lowers her eyes down to my cock. "Maybe it does. I'm trying to be practical about the whole thing. You want your memories back, right?"

"Yes."

"And I want you to get them back because I don't think I could—" She stops herself short, and I find myself leaning closer to her on the bed.

"You don't think you could, what?"

She shakes her head. "Nevermind. I'm up to the task if you think you can handle it."

I try not to snort. "Handle it? You are a human female. Anything you give me; I am sure I can take."

"Don't be so confident, Cade. I used to do some things to you that left you waddling for a week." She flashes me a surprisingly toothy grin, and another tickling occurs at the back of my mind. A flash. An image of Dakota, but not as she is now. I blink hard, and Dakota's staring at me with a worried expression. "You okay?"

"I just… I think something came back to me."

"It did?" Excitement blossoms across her face, but I hold my hands up.

"Not a lot," I say, hating that I must calm her. "But it was something."

"What?"

"You," I said thickly. "I saw you. With others. Other females. The rest of the image is blurry, but in my mind, you were as clear as the day I was exiled. I only saw you." I clasp my forehead. "Scheita, that's weird. I swear I just got the memory, but now it feels as though it's always been there."

"Well… well, don't push it," she stammers, easing me back down on the bed.

"I am fine!" I don't want her to treat me like a helpless sprog. I am Sidyth. I am bigger, stronger, faster, and more potent than this female, and yet she treats me as though I am fragile. "Dakota, stop this," I say in a softer voice, knowing this entire conversation has had way too many ups and downs for either of us to handle without being shaken. "I thought we agreed to push harder to bring some of my memories back."

"Yes, but—"

"You said you wanted to push me," I remind her, resisting the urge to cover that full mouth with my hand.

I may not have any memories of this female in front of me, but I am sure being coddled is probably the last way to stir up some of my lost memories.

"I do, but I don't want you to get hurt."

"I am not so fragile." Losing a bit of patience, I reach out to seize her wrist and pull her to me on the bed. It happens so quickly that she doesn't have time to react. One moment I'm sitting in the bed, and the next, I have her cheek pressed up against my bare chest.

And so help me, Goddess, it feels right to have her here.

She doesn't fight, and I feel myself relaxing. This female may be my mate because I'm surprised at how well she fits against me. Shocked by how calm I feel when her hot, sweaty skin is pressed up against mine. Have we done this before? I am sure we have. Dakota always spoke of snuggling and such, and something feels right.

This female must belong to me.

I pinch my eyes shut and will the memories to come back. I want them so desperately now I can barely stand it. She says she put her lips on my cock. She says I lapped the sweet nectar that came from her cunt. Such things used to make me cringe but holding onto Dakota now makes me wonder if I genuinely did do such a thing and allowed such a thing to happen to me. Females don't do that type of thing on Sidetha, but now I can picture it. Dakota's sweet, sassy mouth wrapped around the crown of my cock and sucking gently. My tongue brushing against the curls covering her slit.

Curls? Where did that idea come from? Sidyth females don't have curls down there. But thinking of Dakota now, nothing else makes sense.

I may not have clear memories of the female I'm holding, but feeling what I'm feeling now, I'll stop at nothing to get them back.

Starting right now.

**The Rebels of Sidyth (and the)
Human Females Who Tame Them**

Information about names, pairings and kiddos as of book nine.

<u>Lair One</u>

Prince Korben – Exiled former prince of the fatherland.
    Blythe – His Chosen. Kind of the leader because she's the 'guinea pig' of the group.
    Kyeth – Their baby girl.

Azan – Prince Korben's universal translator.
    York – His Chosen. Pregnant.
    Yazrik – Their baby boy.

Hujun – Prince Korben's bodyguard.
    Ellis – His Chosen.
    Junis – Their baby boy. Large and likes to punch.

Dolan – Azan's little brother.
    Layla – His Chosen.
    Dyela – Their baby girl. Very small.

Exer – Former spy on the fatherland.
    Sloane – His Chosen.
    Rexlan – Twin Boy #1
    Exlo – Twin Boy #2

Drazal – Keeps watch over Phoebe.
    Phoebe – Drazal's Chosen Mate. Newly Pregnant.

Glykoran – Main watcher of the lair opening. Widower.
  Celeste – His Chosen mate.

Iriel – Exiled from Prince Korben's lair for bothering the females.

Lacey – Can't stand any of the Sidyths.
  Aoi –
  Krista – Close friends with Celeste. No interest in a mate.
  Rhyan –

Taylis – Mated to Alaska
  Chocal – Newcomer. Mysterious and connected to Drazal somehow.
  Drozass – Mated to Arizona
  Dash – Pleasure mate with Kansas.
  Cade – Pleasure mate with Dakota

The State Girls:

Arizona – Leader of the State Girls; mated to Drozass
  Alaska – Second Leader of the State Girls; mated to Taylis
  Kansas – Newest Member of the State Girls
  Dakota – Member of the State Girls

The Workout Twins:

Rene –
  Devyn –

<u>Lair Two:</u>

Taya – Youngest human female on assignment.

Adrienne (Drey) –

Mia – Enjoys messing with Iriel. Calls him 'little mermaid'.

Wixlass – Youngest male at the secondary lair.

Chentan – Only Sidyth with Human medical information.

Dedication

I can't write without readers.

I thank you so much for

taking the time to read my book.

I wouldn't be able to do this for

a living if it weren't for you guys.

Thank you so much for

reading *Tamed by the Alien!*

About the Author

Sabrina Kade lives in Pittsburgh, Pennsylvania and enjoys everything Christmas, shoujo manga, and old Hollywood movies Her life is surprisingly normal with her husband and two beautiful daughters, and despite what she writes, she enjoys evenings at home with her family with good food, good drinks, and a good night's rest. And while she does enjoy dirty science fiction, she finds as much enjoyment with clean reads with happy endings as she does with the darkest of horror stories.

If you liked this story, you might like some of my other books. You can join my mailing list by dropping by my website https://sabrinakade.wordpress.com/newsletter/ or if you have any comments, shoot me a note at sabrinakade@sabrinakade.com I am always happy to hear from people who've read my work. I try to answer every email I receive.

If you liked *Tamed by the Alien,* please tell any of your friends who enjoy sass, sex, and a side of sci-fi. Also, please leave a review! I much appreciate any kind words, even one or two sentences go a long way. The number of reviews an eBook receives significantly improves how well an eBook does on Amazon.

Amazon – https://www.amazon.com/author/sabrinakade
BookBub – https://www.bookbub.com/authors/sabrina-kade

Other Titles by Sabrina Kade

Rebels of Sidyth

Educated by the Alien

Purchased by the Alien

Guarded by the Alien

Promised to the Alien

Demanded by the Alien

Desired by the Alien

Abducted by the Alien

Committed to the Alien

Addicted to the Alien

Tamed by the Alien

Enticed by the Alien

Compelled by the Alien

Cherished by the Alien

Chosen Narratives

Never Blamed

Never Tamed

Never Ashamed

Claimed by the Alien Guard

9 798663 977425